"You're C...
Righ...

"Robert Innes, put me down!" Carol Anne kicked and struggled until he set her down on her feet. But he immediately picked up her two suitcases and marched off. She looked frantically around, seeking help, but Robert was out of sight. By the time she reached him he was already tossing her bags into the back of his station wagon.

"Get in the car!" he ordered.

"Swine!" She breathed deeply. "Give me back my luggage."

Robert marched toward her and scooped her up in his arms like a baby. Then he got the car door open and dropped her on the front seat.

"Now stay there!" he roared.

PAULA FULFORD,
born in Spain, now resides in Toronto, Canada. The works of John Steinbeck and Somerset Maugham were influential in her choice of careers. She readily admits that she always wanted to write "even when it seemed it could be only for my own amusement."

Dear Reader:

Silhouette Romances is an exciting new publishing venture. We will be presenting the very finest writers of contemporary romantic fiction as well as outstanding new talent in this field. It is our hope that our stories, our heroes and our heroines will give you, the reader, all you want from romantic fiction.

Also, *you* play an important part in our future plans for Silhouette Romances. We welcome any suggestions or comments on our books and I invite you to write to us at the address below.

So, enjoy this book and all the wonderful romances from Silhouette. They're for *you!*

Karen Solem
Editor-in-Chief
Silhouette Books
P. O. Box 769
New York, N.Y. 10019

PAULA FULFORD
Island Destiny

Silhouette **Romance**

Published by Silhouette Books New York

SILHOUETTE BOOKS, a Simon & Schuster Division of
GULF & WESTERN CORPORATION
1230 Avenue of the Americas, New York, N.Y. 10020

ISBN: 0-671-57020-X

First Silhouette printing July, 1980

10 9 8 7 6 5 4 3 2 1

Island
Destiny

Chapter One

"How would you like to spend a few days in Jamaica?"

Carol Anne Todd looked at Mr. Roxlet, her boss, without understanding what he was saying. She had been sitting at her desk watching the snowflakes whirling past the office window. Ice had formed on the inside of the windows, around the edges of the frames. It all looked very Christmassy, but it was still only November. More than five months of this dreary sort of weather loomed ahead in winter-bound Toronto. Carol Anne Todd was in the process of feeling very sorry for herself when Mr. Roxlet spoke.

"I'm sorry; say that again?"

"I was wondering if you'd like to spend a week in a brand-new hotel, sunbathing by a sparkling pool, sipping fruit-flavored drinks and being wined and dined by handsome, elegant young men. But of course, if you're not interested, I can always get—"

"Now, wait a minute, Mr. Roxlet! Just because I was doing a little daydreaming doesn't mean to say I wasn't listening. You asked if I'd like to go to Jamaica for a week, right?"

"Right."

"So, right; this time I heard you. I want to go to Jamaica; who do I have to shoot?"

Mr. Roxlet laughed out loud, tilting his head back. "No, Carol Anne, no," he said at last. "This is business." He sat down in the chair in front of Carol Anne's desk, just like a customer. His face was serious when next he spoke.

"Carol Anne, ours is the fastest-growing travel agency in Canada. We've built our reputation on a number of things, and one of them has been the way we've been able to take new hotels and guest houses and promote them so that they become popular with Canadians. What we've done has helped make Barbados almost another Canadian province; more Canadians go there than people of any other nationality. We've almost done as much with Bermuda. And now it's Jamaica's turn. This is the year we're pushing Jamaica as a Canadian travel spot, as you already know." He broke into a smile, raised his forefinger and unconsciously waved it at Carol Anne.

"Jamaica is going to boom! It's past its troubles now, and sooner or later it's going to be the 'in' spot in the entire Caribbean. And we're getting in on the ground floor."

"But what's that got to do with me? How can I help?"

"By going to Jamaica! Just like I asked you."

"I'll go, I'll go! When?"

"Carol Anne, let's be serious now." Mr. Roxlet dropped his waving forefinger and his smile; he became strictly business. "You're a clever, innovative girl. When you took over our accounts department, it was a mess, as I know only too well. I'll admit it cost us a few dollars to send you to that accounting firm with our problems, but it paid off. The ideas you brought back with you have straightened out the problems, and—"

"But all I did was what they said I ought to!"

"Maybe so. But the fact is that it was you who did it, when there were others of us here who should have and didn't. So that's initiative, in my book, and initiative is a quality that's sadly lacking today. So when a company like

8

ours finds it, we're willing to back it—to a reasonable extent, of course.

"Carol Anne, you're young yet, but you're smart. Stick with us and you'll go places. There's no place a clever woman *can't* go, these days, in business. You're smart and you've got ideas, and what's more, you've got a sense of humor. Now that you're out of the accounts department and you're a licensed travel agent, it's time you started using your talents to get ahead in the mainstream of this business. I don't know if you're aware of it, but the travel agency business is presently going through the greatest growth rate of any business in all of history, and you're in on the ground floor. Who knows how you might end up? Why, just the ideas you gave us for the new brochure on the Inverurie Hotel in Bermuda were worth thousands to us! And you've never even been to Bermuda."

"I've never even been *anywhere!* I've only been in the travel agency division a month."

"All the more reason for you to start traveling now, and stop worrying about it, because I'm going to tell you something: This is no big, terribly important job I'm sending you on; it's just a little job. It doesn't matter if you make it or break it.

"What's happened is that some place calling itself the Innes estate in Jamaica has decided to turn their main house into a hotel. By the sound of it I'd guess it's going to be more of a guest house than a hotel. They want us to represent them in Canada and the northern United States, so they've asked us to prepare a brochure and plan a promotional campaign for them. They'd like to have some sort of grand opening, too, if we can come up with a good gimmick to pin it on, and they've asked us to send somebody down to look the place over and give them a few tips; it seems they've not been in the hotel business before, and could use some help in getting set up.

"It's all perfectly straightforward. I'll give you our

9

standard questionnaire covering new hotels. You fill it out when you've looked the place over. Get to know the owners; see what they think. If they're missing any of the usual things, like a pool or a bar, tell them they'll need them. Have them get in touch with an architect if they need such things installed. Just go down there, keep your eyes open, fill in the questionnaire, give them a few hints—which I'm sure your quick young mind will come up with—and while you're at it, take a few days off and get a suntan."

Mr. Roxlet got out of his chair, beaming on Carol Anne. "I'd like you to get down there within the next couple of days. So pack a bag, phone your mother to let her know where you'll be, make yourself out a ticket and charge it to the promotional expense account, and away you go."

Before she could think of an answer, Mr. Roxlet had left. Carol Anne's hand reached instinctively for the phone. She simply had to tell *someone* the tremendous news at once. Who first?

She wasn't given time to decide. Mr. Roxlet was back, carrying an envelope from which he was pulling a printed form.

"It's amazing the number of people who think running a hotel is just a matter of having some rooms to rent." He put the form on Carol Anne's desk so that she could see it. "People don't realize what else is involved. Staff, bar service, food service, laundry facilities and a thousand other things—they're all here on this list." He tapped the form.

"All you need to do is check for them when you get there, and give them a rating in these spaces. I trust your judgment. But don't forget that this new venture is planned as a resort hotel. Which means that it simply has to have a lot of extras, like sports facilities of all kinds—tennis courts are a must, these days—and certainly they need a pool. But even that won't be enough; there has to be something unique about each successful resort

10

hotel. It could be a view, for instance. Or its location on a mountaintop. Keep your eyes open for something of that nature that we can *sell* in the brochure we'll be putting together—that special something that will be the perfect added attraction for people planning a vacation. And if they haven't got anything unique, don't hesitate to suggest they *build* something. They've got to have it."

"Build what sort of thing, Mr. Roxlet?"

"I mean build on the attractions they already have, rather than adding a building. Perhaps there could be guided tours to some attractive local spot. Or underwater scuba viewing if the sea is close by. Just keep looking, and you'll find it. You're a smart girl, Carol Anne, and I'm counting on you." Mr. Roxlet smiled as he said it. Carol Anne picked up the form and really tried to study it, but her mind was in such a whirl she could hardly see the words.

"My mother won't believe it," she blurted out. "I'll have to phone her right away! I'll have to buy some clothes! Do you really mean it, Mr. Roxlet? When can I leave?"

"Whenever you're ready. Just remember to send a telegram to Adam Innes telling him when you'll be arriving, because the estate is a long way from the airport and he'll have to pick you up."

And after that came two frantic days of phoning mother and friends, buying new swimsuits and suntan oil and sandals and a new long dress in case there was an occasion to wear it and a pair of slingback high-heeled shoes in the latest fashion and packing a suitcase and emptying it all out again in despair; all too soon, yet not soon enough, it was time to go and, with a heart as light as any of the snowflakes whirling about her head, she set out through a fresh new blizzard to the airport.

Chapter Two

It was all so unexpected; all the warm, smiling faces, all the lilting voices, and the riot of colors even in the airport building. And it wasn't anywhere near as hot as Carol Anne had imagined. Instead it was like an Indian-summer day, but with a differently scented air, and just right. So this was Jamaica!

She was curious about all the intriguing odors. There was the smell of cigar smoke. The hint of expensive perfume must waft all the way over from the duty-free shop—or from the beautifully dressed women waiting for their flights to be called. But there were stranger smells—of fruits and exotic flowers, even the wood of the chair she was sitting on had its own distinctive odor.

And the marvelous sounds of the voices! Her ears tried to sort out the meaning from the lilting singsong voices of the people around her. Even the girl who spoke over the public-address system had that singsong tone, and it was especially important to Carol Anne that she be able to understand her, because when she'd inquired if a certain Captain Adam Innes was expecting her, she'd been asked to take a seat and wait till she was paged; it seemed Mr. Innes had phoned to say he'd be late. So every time the speakers came to life, Carol Anne sat up straighter to listen.

Her nose, her ears, and especially her eyes were taking it all in. She put on her sunglasses so that she could stare at people without being obvious.

The clothes! How smart and expensive-looking the women were. She mentally cataloged her own outfit: spanking-new white sling-backed high-soled shoes, with a white pocketbook that had a diagonal blue stripe across it, her best summer dress, a one-piece sleeveless lavender cotton, form-fitting and knee-length, under that a new wine-colored lingerie set. She wore no hat, and her only jewelry was a brooch which had been her mother's; it clipped together both ends of a blue silk scarf which was loose around her long neck. Carol Anne knew she looked cool and neat, and the sunglasses made her feel very mysterious and cosmopolitan. She only hoped her hair was still behaving. She'd brushed the silky brown mass before she got off the plane, and it hung loose and free, cascading softly over her shoulders.

Cool and neat, that's me, she told herself confidently just as a large and dusty young man strode past her, walking as if he owned the airport, adding a new scent to the ones already tickling her nose. He was wearing khaki shorts and a once-white open-neck shirt, and he was looking all the girls over as if he meant to have one of them as soon as he had time. She couldn't help smiling at the sight. He glanced at her too, and frowned, but unexpectedly brought his hand up to a half-salute as he marched on. Safe behind her sunglasses, Carol Anne winked at his broad back. Handsome hunk, she thought, but grubby; he looked as if he'd been rolling on the ground somewhere. Much too sure of himself, though, for my taste. But he was certainly handsome. Tall, but with such broad shoulders that he didn't look tall except when he strode with long, purposeful steps past an ordinary man, and only then was it obvious that he was big. And the muscles of him, displayed with uncaring ease everywhere that his skimpy shorts and thin shirt didn't cover, rippled and flowed like those of a racehorse.

13

No, not a racehorse, Carol Anne told herself disdainfully, a wild mustang that needs civilizing with rope and bridle and whip too, if need be. He looks too wild to be trusted among thoroughbreds.

Caught up in her own imagination, she couldn't keep her eyes off him, but watched his dark head while, without actually touching anyone, he marched in a perfectly straight line and without slackening pace directly to where he intended.

Arrogant, that's the word for him, thought Carol Anne. She watched him make his way through to the ticket counter, looking very active and purposeful; all the beautifully dressed people immediately gave him way. He wore knee-length dusty white socks and his shoes could have been any color, they were so soiled, and when he got to the counter he slapped both pants pockets before looking for something in them, raising a double cloud of dust. She was glad to be sitting at a safe distance; her neat and cool look would rapidly disintegrate in a dust storm like that. But he was certainly an attractive-looking man, with brawny brown arms and knees as if he spent much of his time working under the Jamaican sun. He might be cute if someone gave him a bath.

The public-address system came to life again, and this time it was her name that was called out, asking her to report to the ticket counter. Carol Anne started to her feet with a racing heart, wishing she'd taken time to look in her pocketbook mirror to check if her hair was behaving itself.

She walked demurely to the counter, trying to look the very picture of a professional travel agent doing her thing, while desperately peering through her glasses in an effort to pick out Captain Adam Innes from among the crowd of people gathered around the counter. Perhaps it was that nice-looking older man with the panama hat. Or that young man with the mustache.

But it was the dusty one. He gave her a half-bow, unsmiling, very formal and old-fashioned, and didn't take her extended hand to shake. Carol Anne felt quite unwelcome, and for the first time since she'd set out on this assignment she felt like a fraud, as if she was here under false pretenses.

But she wasn't a fraud, she was just new at the job, she reminded herself indignantly. Even if this was her first overseas assignment, she was still a bona-fide travel agent; everyone has to start sometime, so why should she feel guilty?

"I'm Robert Innes, of the Innes estate, and I'm sorry to be late, but there was a problem on the estate that had to be attended to before I could leave. Is that your luggage over there? Good. Now, if you'll just follow me." His voice was low and businesslike.

He marched off carrying both suitcases, one in his hand and the other tucked under his arm like a newspaper. Carol Anne recalled struggling with the weight of those cases in Toronto only a few hours ago and marveled at his strength. But why did he dislike her? She could feel a definite antipathy flowing from him as she followed his broad back. He made no effort to let her walk by his side.

And he was so quiet. He didn't speak another word. Outside, under the full strength of the sun, it was a great deal hotter. Innes led the way to an old station wagon that was as grubby as he himself—so dusty it was hard to say what color it was. Carol Anne almost stopped right then, panicking at what this was going to do to her best summer dress. But Innes was already putting her cases through the back window, then coming around to her side to open her door for her. She looked inside in dismay; the seat was thick with dust, but Mr. Innes made no move to do anything about it. And suddenly Carol Anne was determined he shouldn't get the idea that she was too dainty and ladylike to ride in his old car.

Resolutely she stepped inside and sat down, repressing the instinctive shudder.

Innes walked around the front and got behind the wheel—which she suddenly noticed was on the wrong side of the car; then she remembered reading that in Jamaica people drove on the left side of the road. That must explain it. She decided to say nothing about it. If she did, perhaps Robert Innes would think she wasn't used to being in foreign countries, and that would never do for a travel agent. Instead, still in silence, she forced herself to relax against the backrest, knowing full well that her dress was now completely ruined.

He started the car with a thunderous roar that jolted Carol Anne upright in terror.

"Sorry about that," Innes shouted over the noise.

"What did you say?" Carol Anne cupped an ear to listen.

"The muffler!" he bellowed back as he put the car into gear. "It fell off on the way here. I'll have to fix it before we go back!"

They drove away from the airport in sonorous grandeur, with Carol Anne so embarrassed she wished she had the courage to lie on the floor so that nobody could see her. When they reached the narrow, winding road that led into Kingston, all the little children came out to wave and cheer and shout unheard advice to Mr. Innes, telling him what he should do about his muffler. The vibrating car raised the dust from its upholstery, floating it all over Carol Anne's good clothes in a thin film. Deafened and dust-covered, Carol Anne was suddenly engulfed in homesickness. Had it only been this morning that she'd left nice, safe, cold Toronto? She fell into a daydream filled with self-pity, but the thunder of the unmuffled car exhaust was dying down to a grumbling cough, bringing Carol Anne out of her homesick reverie and back to hot and noisy reality. She sat up straight to look about her, glancing at the stern profile of the man who was driving. Cold-blooded type, she thought, but handsome.

They were pulling up at a garage in the residential part of Kingston. A tall black man who seemed to be the garage owner was coming toward the old station wagon.

"Good to see you, Robert," he called out as Innes got out of the car. "I can guess what you're in here for."

A young boy was following the owner. He came around to the back of the wagon and took out Carol Anne's suitcases as she got out herself. Robert Innes spoke.

"You can go with that boy, miss, while the car's being fixed. He'll show you where you can freshen up. We should be all set to go in about an hour, so be ready." And without another word he was gone, following the owner into the garage. There was nothing Carol Anne could do but follow the boy who was carrying her suitcases inside the large house next door to the garage.

It was obviously someone's home, but there was only a maid inside it to greet her. She showed Carol Anne to the bathroom upstairs.

It was delightfully cool in the house, air-conditioned, Carol Anne guessed. There must be a lot of money in the service-station business here in Jamaica. It was so cool she realized she had been perspiring, and when she looked at herself in the long bathroom mirror she could have cried. Her dress was a mess. Its color was now a streaky beige, and so were her shoes. She could hardly tell where the blue stripe began or ended on her pocketbook because it was so dirty. And all this in just the short ride from the airport. What will I look like after riding all the way out to the estate itself?

Grimly she peeled off her clothes and shook them, then stopped, fearing to make a mess of the spotless bathroom. She folded them instead. A bath, she told herself. No, a shower; it's faster. But my poor hair. What can I do about it in just one hour?

She glared at it in the mirror. It still looked reasonably smooth and straight, falling over her shoulders, except for one thick strand that had sneaked away to fall over her left eye. She blew it away out of the corner of her mouth, then, when it fell back, swept it fiercely away with her hand. At once her hand encountered dust. She ran all her

17

fingers through her hair, pulling at the snarls, ready to cry with frustration and disappointment.

"Thirty dollars!" she moaned. "I paid thirty dollars only yesterday at the hairdresser's. And now look at it!"

That awful man! He must have known this would happen. What right had he to be so domineering and rough? What had she done to make him hate her? Or was he just, plainly and simply, a swine?

"Mr. Innes, you are a swine, grade A," she told her reflection between clenched teeth. Her long face looked fierce; her dark brown eyes sparkled. She laughed at herself and stepped back to study herself.

Long and slender, like her face. Good, trim figure, and clean, smooth skin. Nothing spectacular, she told herself, but not that bad, either. So why does that man hate me? Not that he's such a charmer. Too heavily built, for one thing; probably fat in places where his clothes cover it. Too strong an aura of . . . What? Power? Confidence? Whatever it was, he was overdoing it. Someone would have to do something about him before he was fit to have around.

But not me, she told herself. That's not going to be my job. Let someone else tame him, she added as she got the shower running.

After she was dry, she combed her hair, tugging at the snarls, drowning in homesickness. She had a very clear vision of her own tiny bathroom in her apartment, and of herself luxuriating in the overflowing tub, her hair lathered into a great white glob of shampoo.

She cleaned up the bathroom as best she could before she got dressed again. Then she went through her suitcase, looking for the right things to wear, finally settling on a pair of tennis shorts and a new soft yellow cotton shirt. They'd get dirty too before she got to wherever she was going, but they were meant to get dirty and could be washed easily.

She didn't have any knee-length socks like Mr. Innes

was wearing, so rather than wear short ones, she rummaged in her case for her sandals to complete the outfit. Finally she took her blue silk scarf and made a bandana out of it. She looked at herself in the mirror.

"Carol Anne Todd," she told herself coldly, "you look like something the cat found and dragged home." Then she burst into a giggle, surprising herself. No doubt about it, she did look weird. The scarf was definitely wrong. She took it off, shaking her hair loose. It couldn't get any worse, she reasoned, so why not let it fly in the wind?

This time she folded the scarf, then tied it fairly tightly around her long neck, with a loose knot just under one ear. There, that's a little better, she told her reflection.

She freshened her lipstick, then put on her sunglasses just as the maid came upstairs to tell her it was time to go.

"Now, Mr. Innes, do your worst; you and your old car both," Carol Anne said under her breath as she went out into the bright afternoon sunshine. She fixed a large cheerful smile on her face that was as sunny as the sun itself.

But it was wasted; Robert Innes hardly glanced at her. He just took her suitcases from the boy and threw them into the back of the wagon, then went around and opened the door for Carol Anne without a word.

She was determined to take no notice of his rudeness. Maybe he has some secret sorrow or something, she told herself. Perhaps someone was nasty to him over breakfast this morning and he hasn't gotten over it yet. Whatever it is, he's got more important things on his mind than being nice to little old me. But I'm not going to let that worry me. See if I care.

Glowing with a sense of righteousness and antagonism, Carol Anne held her nose in the air as she stepped into the car. She settled into her seat. Then she gasped.

"Why, the car's been washed!"

"It needed it. So I got it done after the muffler was fixed." He slammed closed her door and walked around the front of the car to his own seat, sliding in and starting the motor. He backed away with a rush, threw the car into drive, and shot forward, jerking Carol Anne against her seat. She gritted her teeth. If he was going to drive like this . . .

But as soon as they were out in the road, he drove more calmly. She relaxed a little.

"It's a long drive, Miss Todd, so make yourself comfortable."

For the first time since she'd met him, Robert Innes looked directly at her as he spoke, and Carol Anne saw that his eyes were exactly the same color blue as the scarf she'd tied around her neck. It quite unsettled her. She didn't know exactly what she said in reply as a consequence, but she hoped it was something appropriately forgiving. Those very blue eyes in that tanned face! Just like Lawrence of Arabia when Peter O'Toole played him in that movie. Mrs. Innes must be very watchful over him or half the girls in Jamaica would fall for him.

They drove off the side street and onto a main road leading out of town toward the nearby mountains. Carol Anne peeked sideways and tried to see if her companion was in a talking mood or not. She couldn't tell. Robert Innes just drove, concentrating on the road, not looking her way at all. His nose is very straight, she thought, and his eyebrows are very thick and black, just like his hair. Black hair, brown skin, straight nose, and his name is Robert Innes. . . .

Robert Innes? She sat up straight.

But it was a Mr. Adam Innes she was supposed to meet at the airport! In fact, when Mr. Roxlet, the travel agency manager, had told her about him, he'd mentioned that he was "Captain" Adam Innes.

"Is Captain Adam Innes your brother?" Carol Anne blurted out.

Robert Innes looked away from the road a moment to answer.

"The Captain? No, he's my father. And the hotel is his

20

idea, not mine. He was supposed to come pick you up today, but he hurt his arm, so I had to."

His manner was curt, his voice low, and he spoke as if he hated having to speak at all and wanted to get it over with. He kept his gaze fixed on the road ahead while he spoke.

Carol Anne felt very small and unwanted, like a kitten on a strange doorstep in a rainstorm. The way he'd spoken made it clear that he didn't care for the idea of a hotel on his father's estate and wanted nothing to do with it. Accordingly he resented her for being a part of it, and resented even more having had to drop his own work and come to pick her up at the airport. It left her in an unpleasant predicament, for after all, she had been sent down here to find out what she could about the very thing he didn't want to talk about. She tried to find the right words to ask her next question, but gave up. Finally she just asked what was on her mind.

"Tell me about the hotel," she said at last, her heart filled with misgivings.

He just grunted. For a while it looked as if that was the only answer she was going to get. But then he spoke.

"There isn't one. We have a huge old manor house on the estate that's sitting practically empty, so the Captain wants to turn it into a hotel. He's had a pool built and made a few alterations, and now he's asked your agency to send someone down to look it over." He glanced sideways for a long moment at Carol Anne, his face expressionless. She felt the color rising to her cheeks. Doesn't he think I'm capable?

"The only good thing about it is that it'll keep the Captain busy and leave me free to concentrate on the farms, which are really all that count; everything else is secondary."

So, she thought, do I detect a protective feeling toward these farms? Better be careful.

"Whereabouts is this manor house?"

"I suppose you do have a right to know. Our estate is on

21

the far side of Mandeville, heading toward the south coast, in a long valley with a low hill rising out of one end, and the manor house is built on it. It's just the old estate house. It's huge, all right; been in the family for years, and every generation has added to it."

Surprisingly his voice had grown softer while he described his home. Even more surprisingly, he chuckled, and continued without Carol Anne having to ask him anything.

"The first Innes built it. Only, his name wasn't Innes, but Iñez. That was about three hundred years ago. It seems Captain Iñez was given a land grant here when he was invalided out of the Spanish navy, instead of being given passage home. Rumor has it that he already had a wife and many children in Spain, but he took up with a local woman anyway and founded our family."

He chuckled again at some private joke, then fell silent, concentrating while he negotiated the first curve leading up into the mountains.

Carol Anne held her tongue and waited for him to pick up the thread again. But as the minutes passed and he remained silent, she realized she'd need to prime the pump once more if she wanted to get the words flowing again.

But she felt timid. In his mood, Robert Innes was almost bound to snap at anything she said. But she had to find out.

"The idea of a hotel in a three-hundred-year-old manor house is very appealing," she said at last, almost as if to herself, but glancing at Robert to make sure he had heard.

"A glorified guest house," he said shortly.

"It depends on how it's furnished, and if it—"

"It will have to be just as it is," he cut in. "The Captain has already spent a fortune on the pool and his remodeling, and it has to be enough. It has to pay its own way."

Aha, thought Carol Anne. Money. That's the problem. Now she felt more confident.

"Well, we can worry about that after I've seen it," she

soothed him. "But tell me about the farms. They sound very big."

"They are big. Used to be bigger. Right now we still have fifteen hundred acres. At one time it used to be all in sugarcane, but the bottom dropped out of that market years ago, so now it's mixed crops. Still depends on sugar, though."

"Did you sell off some of the land?"

"My father did. But now I'm looking after the farms, and they're going to pay." There was a note of fierce pride in his voice, as if he was daring the world to argue with him. Carol Anne added this fact to her growing store of knowledge.

And while she was doing so, it was suddenly night. Just as if someone had switched off the sun. She gasped. One minute it had been bright daylight, but now it was velvety dark. She could already see bright stars burning, millions of them.

Robert Innes switched the car headlights on. Carol Anne looked at her watch. Six-thirty. It hardly seemed decent, this sudden onrush of darkness; even in the middle of a Toronto winter it stayed light for quite a while after the sun went down.

Robert Innes surprised her by laughing again; he had a pleasant laugh, soft and deep. "Tropical nights come quickly," he told her. "It's because we're nearer to the equator."

"That's true," she agreed, trying to understand.

She settled herself farther back in her seat, listening to the now bearable hum of the motor, watching the bright bugs flashing to their doom against the bespattered windshield in the glare of the headlights as the car rushed through the unknown darkness.

This Robert Innes was quite a grump, she was thinking. Mention the hotel—which is why she was here in Jamaica in the first place—and he became downright nasty. Acted as if she'd come here just to annoy him. She felt defenseless in face of his attitude. He was such a big,

23

powerful, forceful man, and his mind was evidently completely made up against her and the job she'd been sent to do. She closed her eyes, feeling lost.

The car rode smoothly and quietly; it was soothing to her apprehensions to just sit there and not have to talk, to just be carried into the night by the car with its confident, competent driver. Normally she was ill-at-ease when somebody else was driving, much preferring to drive herself, but somehow she felt secure with Robert Innes driving. He might be unpleasant, but he just exuded calm confidence. He certainly felt sure of himself.

And he did have a nice laugh. There must be another side to him besides his unpleasant one. He must really hate the idea of turning his ancestral home into a hotel; and in a way she could sympathize with that attitude. But, even so, it wasn't her fault; it hadn't been her idea.

It wasn't fair, his acting as if it was all her fault. Suddenly she asked him outright, "Why are you so dead set against having a hotel on your estate? Surely anyone would be glad of the extra income and the new people a hotel would bring into their lives, so why are you so much against it?"

Again, for some moments, he didn't talk. But when he did, his voice was cold and hard, making her wish she hadn't asked him.

"How would you like it if someone turned your own home into a rooming house? How would you like it if, despite all your best efforts and hardest work, your own father told you it wasn't enough and the only way to make ends meet is to take in boarders—"

"But that isn't the way it would be at all!" she broke in, but it only made his voice rise when he answered.

"I don't care to discuss it. You can just accept that I'm totally against the idea and leave it at that."

He frightened her. Words crowded to the tip of her tongue to answer him with, but they were alone in this car, and miles and miles from anywhere or anyone as far as she

24

knew, and he was angry already. There was no telling what he might do if she argued with him.

So, angry herself by now, she kept silent, and the miles passed that way, with only the sound of the car for company.

She had become so confident of Robert's driving that she'd stopped paying attention to the road ahead and was almost dozing instead. For mile after mile there'd been nothing but the yellow circle of light on the dark road surface, framed by the black night all round them. There had not been any traffic, nor any pedestrians, so it took more than a moment for the sudden appearance of a four-legged creature larger than a big dog in the glare of the lights to register in her mind.

The animal was squarely in their path. Blinded and frightened by the lights, it charged toward them at the same moment that Robert stepped hard on the brake, cursing and leaning on the horn.

They had been traveling at close to fifty miles an hour. If the animal hadn't been racing toward them, Robert might have been able to stop before hitting it.

Carol Anne still hadn't fully comprehended what was taking place; it was all happening too fast. She was thrown against the door as Robert swung the wheel hard over in a desperate effort to miss the terrified beast; the squeal of the tires sounded like a scream of terror.

And during the duration of that scream, as if in slow motion, she saw the animal come closer and closer, recognized it as a donkey with ears flattened back and mouth wide open to bray as it raced toward them. Then with a ghastly thunk the donkey hit the hood over the left wheel, flipped over onto its back in a somersault to land on the car roof and slid off it to the rear as the station wagon finally came to a halt.

Robert was out of the car at once, leaving his door swinging. Carol Anne sat dazed. The roof of the car directly over her head was squashed downward a few inches. The windshield in front of her had shattered into a starburst. The headlight on her side was pointing up into the sky, shining toward the stars.

Shakily she got out, opening the door with difficulty because it had partly jammed.

She couldn't see Robert in the gloom behind the car, but she could hear the hoarse gasping of the donkey. It was in the bottom of the roadside ditch, lying on its side, struggling to get up. Robert was sitting on its head, preventing it from moving too much as he felt the animal's ribs carefully, prodding and pushing and watching the donkey to see if a broken bone made it react.

Robert looked up. "I can't find any broken bones, thank heaven. The poor beast is just terrified. I'd better hold her here until she's calmed down."

Carol Anne made her way down into the ditch.

"Watch out; stay clear of her feet—she may kick," he said as he stroked the donkey's neck now, speaking softly to the animal. Little by little it gave up its attempts to rise; soon only the rhythmically heaving flanks showed movement. Carol Anne stood by fascinated and helpless.

"Isn't there anything I can do?" she whispered.

"No. Just keep calm. Don't excite her. I can't take a chance on letting her up yet." He looked directly at her. "Can you drive?" She nodded. "Would you mind moving the car off the road?" She nodded again, scrambling up the bank, glad to have the chance to do something useful.

When she'd parked the car and switched off the main lights, leaving the side lights on in case any traffic came by, she almost tiptoed back to where Robert was.

The donkey was on her feet now. Robert stood by her head, holding her ear, still stroking her neck, speaking soothingly to her.

What a strange man. So sure of himself and confident. So self-centeredly intent on his own affairs. Yet here he was in the middle of the night, down in a muddy ditch giving help to some animal that could almost have killed him by its very stupidity, not half an hour ago. Was it only half an hour? She couldn't tell. It might have been much longer.

What would Mr. Roxlet think if he knew where she was and what she was doing right now? Was this one of the situations he was so sure she could handle?

"Is it all right?" she called down softly.

He didn't answer for a while, not until he had scrambled up the bank and was by her side. His face was very clear in the starlight, and he was smiling when he turned to her.

"Looks like she'll be fine. Healthy little filly," he announced, then smiled.

They watched in silence for a while.

"I don't think she'll move from here. Somebody will find her in the morning," said Robert. "She's quite safe now. We'd better go; it's still a long drive."

Nevertheless he seemed reluctant to leave the animal. "She's a young beast. It was pure luck she didn't get killed when we hit her."

"Your car is damaged, but it still goes. Your side of the windshield is fine, but my side looks like a big glass spiderweb. And one of the headlights points straight up."

He turned to her at last, looking her over. "How about you? Are you hurt at all?"

"No, I'm fine." But exactly at the moment she said it Carol Anne realized she wasn't; she was far from fine. She was suddenly dizzy as a spinning Frisbee as reaction to what had just happened hit her like an avalanche. She was desperately afraid she might faint. Without thinking, she reached out her arms for support.

And Robert reached out his.

She fell weakly into his arms, fighting back tears she didn't understand, clinging to him so that she wouldn't fall, and yet aware enough to be amazed at how rocklike and comforting he was.

"There, there," he said softly, over and over. And as she fought away the feeling of faintness, she realized that he had soothed the little donkey in precisely the same tone

27

of voice. And he had soothed the donkey *first*. She, a human being, wasn't as important to him as an animal! She would have given years off her life to have been able to push herself upright and free right then and there and face him aristocratically and confidently. But she was too weak and shivery to move, and his arms around her were so steady and calming, the earthy smell of his shirt under her face so normal and comforting, that instead of finding herself getting steadier, Carol Anne discovered she was even weaker—quite unable to move—afraid that if he let her go she would fall to the ground. She hadn't the strength to fight the strange feeling.

And, she realized, she didn't want to. It was heavenly to be held like this. She felt herself being guided toward the car, put into her seat. And then the comforting arms left her, and all at once it was deep dark night again, and lonely.

She was aware of him walking around the car to the driver's seat, minutely aware of him getting in, starting the engine, getting the car back on the road. He didn't say anything. But had *he* been aware of how much it had affected her when his arms were around her? She tried to peek at his face without him noticing, her heart beating rapidly, hoping desperately that he hadn't noticed how much the last few minutes had affected her. But she couldn't tell.

He was his old self again, sure and silent, composed and calm. The eyes over the straight nose stared into the gloom ahead, squinting a little on account of the glare of the headlight shining upward.

"Don't worry," he said without looking at her. "There can't be two donkeys wandering loose on this road in any one night; we've already met ours." Then he turned and smiled at her, the smile of a partner, of a companion in arms. Carol Anne settled back against her seat.

Robert Innes. She pondered the name. What sort of man was Robert Innes? Already she thought she was

28

beginning to know, and the measure of him was good. Robert Innes must be a good man, she told herself, and felt a warmth at the admission that surprised her. She remonstrated with herself. Yes, he's a good man, and attractive too, but he's a stranger and he's going to stay a stranger; you're here to do a job, and that's all.

But, somewhere deeper in her heart, a small voice argued differently, and despite all she could do, Carol Anne listened to it. You could easily fall in love with Robert Innes, it said. Angrily she folded her arms and settled back in her seat.

They drove for almost two hours. Carol Anne dozed, waking with a start every time she felt herself sliding sideways. More than once, as her head felt heavier with sleep, she found herself looking longingly at the bronzed, short-sleeved arm of her traveling companion, thinking how cozy it would be if only she could rest her head against that shoulder.

It was cooler now that it was dark and the car was climbing into the hills; she could feel the warmth of him, and her nose was aware of his smell. She'd noticed it first when he passed her in the airport building. It was an earthy, horsey smell, not at all unpleasant even though there was a hint of sweat in it.

Such a strange man. Such a combination of attractions and repulsions. Such a nice laugh, and a very pleasant smile. But all she had to do was mention her reason for being here—the hotel—and he clammed right up and became gruff and rude.

She sighed, her head nodding again, trying desperately to stay awake. Or at least to sleep in an upright position.

Chapter Three

Carol Anne was fast asleep, cozy and comfortable when Robert Innes drew up slowly at the head of the driveway in front of the manor house.

"Miss Todd, we're here. Time to wake up." He shook her gently, letting his hand rest on her arm.

Through a cloud of marshmallows Carol Anne heard his voice. Her eyes blinked open. Blushing furiously, she sat up at once. "I'm so sorry. I didn't mean to lie on your shoulder . . ."

"No apologies needed; it's late, so you must be tired." Robert got out of the car. There was a tiny black man dressed all in white, with a huge, moonlit smile, holding open the door on Carol Anne's side.

"This is Watson," said Robert. "He'll show you up to your room. If you'll just follow him now, he'll take your cases, and if you're hungry he'll bring you up something to eat. Get a good night's sleep. See you tomorrow."

And with that Robert was gone, striding off down the driveway into the night. Carol Anne suddenly felt absolutely alone. Alone and defenseless on an unknown tropical island with only a tiny gnome of a man nodding and smiling and obviously expecting her to follow him up the nearby stairs that led into a huge, dark old house.

There seeming to be no alternative, after a moment's hesitation Carol Anne did just that, though with rising misgivings as she looked about her.

The car was stopped in a courtyard at the head of a slight rise; she could see the driveway descending into the darkness, lit only by three widely spaced tall lamp standards with dim bulbs around which the suicidal moths congregated. Trimmed, flowering shrubs bordered the driveway, and millions of hidden insects within and behind the shrubs chirped and tweeted and made skittering noises. Carol Anne's nose twitched again, just as it had at the airport; there was a sweet and attractive scent in the air, one that she could almost recall having smelled before, but knew she couldn't have. It gave her the strangest feeling of *déjà vu*.

"What is that nice smell?" she asked Watson, who was smiling and waiting at the top of the wooden stairs that led up to a veranda around the large house.

"Frangipani, miss." Watson bobbed his head.

She mounted the steps. They creaked. She looked up, trying to get a clearer view of the old house, but one single floodlight was set above the steps, shining down into her eyes. She hurried to catch up to Watson.

They went through several large, spacious, dimly lit first-floor rooms where all the windows were wide open and a soft night breeze was raising the curtains in an eerie way. Then they came to a grand sweeping, curving staircase, wide enough to carry a grand piano up without having to tilt it. She felt rather regal as she climbed the stairs; Watson had now fallen in behind her, as no doubt he had been trained to do. But at the head of the stairs he took the lead again, flashing the brilliant smile in apology for hurrying past her, moving quickly to throw open the door of a room not too far from the head of the great stairwell. He then bowed slightly as he waited for Carol Anne to precede him, doing so without a break in her stride.

But she stopped dead once she was inside.

The room was enormous. It was far, far bigger than her

31

entire apartment in far-off Toronto. Yet it was so stuffed with furniture that it was cramped. Carol Anne felt awed, and tiny, and overwhelmed.

The walls were lined with floor-to-ceiling armoires, some with mirrors on their doors; enough cupboards to hold the wardrobes of a dozen movie queens. The floor was packed with little tables and soft chairs, with desks and elegant secretarial chairs, with ottomans and with chaise lounges. There were big seats with cushions, and small hard-back chairs with wooden seats; end tables and knickknack tables and even a heavy octagonal card table with all its eight chairs around it.

But the real eye-catcher, the dominant piece of furniture, the most imposing and forbidding thing in the room, was the bed. Mentally Carol Anne capitalized it: The Bed.

Heavens, what a bed! An enormous, overpowering, genuine four-poster with a bloodred canopy overhead and a crimson fringe all the way around it. The canopy looked as if it weighed tons. What if it should come loose and fall on her while she was sleeping? Nobody would hear her screams from under its heavy weight. She'd smother and die under it, like a kitten under a pillow.

"You like?" inquired Watson solicitously. Carol Anne started.

Slowly she turned, with a thousand questions and objections rushing through her head.

"I . . . I'm . . . It's very interesting," she got out at last. Watson smiled from ear to ear in genuine pleasure. He put down her bags on one of the lower tables. They looked like tiny jewels in this setting of massive ancient grandeur.

"Shall I send up a maid to help you unpack, miss?"

Numbly she shook her head, then immediately regretted the instinctive negative, because it would be so comforting to see another woman right now. The thought suddenly went through Carol Anne's head that perhaps the Innes estate was populated solely by men. Obviously

32

this room at least hadn't known a woman's touch in years—perhaps centuries.

"You find the bathroom in there," Watson murmured, indicating a doorway near one of the windows. "Now I take your order for dinner in your room, like Mr. Robert says."

"All right. But I'm not very hungry. Can someone make me up a sandwich or something? And perhaps a glass of milk?"

"Right at once, miss." Watson bowed that quaint half-bow of his and left her alone in the gloomy immensity of her room.

She still stood there, staring around her, unbelieving, very conscious of the chirping and squeaking of the many night insects outside the open windows, and of that jungly, oddly familiar scent of the frangipani flowers. Her nose began to twitch again. She followed it to a window which ran from floor to ceiling, a wide-open narrow window with silken curtains moving in the light breeze, like arms that were beckoning her. It was spooky.

There was a tiny wrought-iron balcony outside the window, with wooden trellises on the walls at each side, and masses of flowering plants growing there. It made the tiny balcony into a bower, charming and ladylike. Carol Anne stepped out into the night, scenting the air. The faintest of cool breezes ruffled her hair, cooling her brow. She looked down into the courtyard, where the station wagon was still parked, floodlit by the light over the steps. She could see the driveway meandering off into the distance, becoming a road through moonlit fields. Lights twinkled in a village about a mile away, and faintly over the distance she could make out the sounds of music.

There was a discreet knock at the door of the room behind her. Reluctantly she turned away from the tranquil night and made her way through the overpowering reality of her room to answer it. Outside stood a nervous maid in a starchy white apron. She could have been about forty, and carried a large silver tray with a gleaming silver tea service on it, also a bowl of exotic fruit, tinkling bone china, toast, marmalade and a plate with a three-decker sandwich. The maid flashed a shy smile, bobbed, hurried in to set the tray on the nearest table, bobbed again and vanished so quickly that she almost seemed to run.

Perhaps I'm the first guest she's ever waited on, thought Carol Anne charitably. Or maybe she's afraid of this room, suggested her subconscious with considerably less charity. Maybe this room's haunted, so the maid hates to stay in it late at . . .

"Be quiet!" said Carol Anne aloud, scaring herself. She looked around to see if anyone had heard, then caught herself at it and giggled.

But it was in a somber mood that she chose one of the more comfortable chairs and sat there eating the three-decker sandwich.. She wondered what her boss, Mr. Roxlet, would think of all this. Somewhere in one of her bags was a printed list, a questionnaire of sorts, that Mr. Roxlet had given her. She was supposed to fill it out, grading all the items with a tick mark as good, fair or bad. There was bound to be a line for accommodation. What should she tick off? Maybe she should just write "spooky" across the spaces where there were supposed to be tick marks. Would Mr. Roxlet understand? She shook her head, reaching for the teapot.

When she lifted it she needed both hands. Solid silver, she decided. How extravagant. She shrugged her shoulders all the way up to her ears.

And that went for all the rest of the furnishings in this room. More than likely every piece was an antique, and possibly valuable; some of the things were really lovely. But it was like looking at a cupful of diamonds and expecting to be overjoyed by their beauty. There were just too many antiques, too crammed together.

And as for that huge, fearsome old bed . . .

Tentatively she tried a tiny spoonful of one of the strange fruits in the bowl. It was delicious; she couldn't even imagine such a taste. So she tried all the fruits, one by one, a little spoonful out of each, and they were all different, all new. There was only one she didn't care for.

After she'd eaten, she puttered around her acres of room, making a great business out of unpacking all her cases, finding just the right place to hang everything in one of the cavernous armoires. Her clothes looked like nothing at all in the vast space. Then she timidly entered the bathroom, expecting to find a large iron bathtub with claw-and-ball feet, and rust under the tap, which surely would be dripping. But instead she was delighted to discover a small, modern, light-green room that smelled of fresh paint and where the plumbing worked as silently and efficiently as ever it did at home. It was obviously newly installed. She spent almost an hour in there, washing her hair and luxuriating in the more familiar surroundings.

But at last she stood in her white night gown, the one with pink bows, at the foot of the big old bed.

She marched determinedly around the bed, threw back the covers, took another deep breath and hopped in, immediately pulling up the covers as far as her wide-open eyes, which stared in fascination at the overhanging, looming bloodred canopy.

Her knuckles gripped the sheet next to her nose. Was the canopy moving? She glared at it, daring it, ready to leap. Her racing mind reminded her of stories she'd read about canopies on four-poster beds that slowly descended during the night and gently smothered the bed's occupants. It was always happening in some ancient inn, run by thieves and cutthroats who murdered innocent travelers for their belongings. And, come to think of it, wasn't this really an ancient inn? Very, very ancient; hundreds of years old. And what did she really know about the people who ran it? That frightened little maid who'd brought in her dinner, for instance; did she know something that Carol Anne didn't? She pulled the bedclothes up a little higher, covering her nose.

And how about that much-too-handsome Robert Innes? *There* was someone who was hiding a secret, if ever there was one. As soon as he'd brought her to this old house, he'd marched off down the dark driveway, off into the night. Where had he gone to? There wasn't anywhere but that quaint village to be seen from her little balcony, so where could he have gone? Surely he wouldn't have walked all the way over to the village when he had the car to ride in. So where was he?

Wouldn't it be nice if he phoned—was there a phone? Or he could whistle from outside her window, or knock on her door, or anything. Really and truly he was the only one she knew here. Just Robert Innes, with the amazing blue eyes. Such an imposing and handsome hunk he was, too. Bright blue eyes and a nice straight nose. And so worried that the hotel would interfere with his farms. Carol Anne decided at once that *nothing* she said or did here would interfere with his old farms. It was a matter of pride. She'd show that good-looking devil that she knew what she was doing. He'd soon find out she was as competent as . . . well, as competent as he himself. More so, perhaps. Because at least she knew what she was supposed to do, but by the way he talked, he wasn't doing too well as a farmer.

And right away she was puzzled. How could such a driving, experienced, hardworking man not do well at whatever he set his mind to doing? It wasn't natural. Could there be some other thing involved that was causing his farms to lose money?

Her training in bookkeeping was aroused; so very often the difference between profit and loss could be found in the way a company kept its accounts. But she sighed and let the thought drift away, telling herself that wasn't why she had been sent down here. No, she was here for very practical reasons, few of which, it appeared, would have much to do with gruff-and-grumpy Mr. Robert Innes.

But he was such a good man. Almost any other person

would have driven on after hitting that donkey, but he didn't.

The little voice from deep inside her heart began to speak to her again. Filled with languorous warmth, Carol Anne listened to it without arguing. She didn't answer or object, she just listened.

It would be easy to fall in love with Mr. Gruff-and-Grumpy, it suggested, and while she listened she drifted away. And before she was aware of it, someone had laid out a bright and sparkling morning for her inspection, all dewy fresh and scented, and the shy little maid from last night was all smiles as she pulled back the curtains to let the sun flood into the room.

Carol Anne was served breakfast out on the very wide veranda, which seemed to run most of the way around the old house at the ground-floor level. It had a roof upheld by carved wooden posts, and there were green awnings lowered partway down to keep out the glare of the morning sun. Up underneath the green awning, close to where Carol Anne was seated, there was an identically colored green lizard, as motionless as a leaf. At first she thought he was carved out of stone and set there as an ornament, but even while she thought it the tiny creature puffed out its yellow throat like a balloon, waiting for some unwary insect to come along and inspect this fascinating yellow bubble, so that it could shoot out its sticky tongue and get breakfast too.

Carol Anne was hypnotized. And while she stared, a hummingbird no bigger than a big bee appeared and flew quite motionless except for the blur of its wings in front of the yellow balloon at the lizard's throat. But in a second the bird realized that this wasn't a flower and vanished instantly. Carol Anne laughed aloud with pleasure. She decided she would make a note of it all for Mr. Roxlet as soon as possible.

There were about a dozen dining tables along the wide

veranda, each with room for six people. All were laid with heavy white tablecloths and silverware. But Carol Anne was the only person there besides the motionless but watchful waiter. Maximum seating capacity, seventy-two people, she noted.

She'd ordered one boiled egg and some toast, but the waiter eventually brought her fresh orange juice, another bowl of the fruits like the ones she'd had in her room last night, mounds of toast and the one egg she'd asked for, plus marmalade and some freshly baked buns in a basket. There was also a heavy pot of strong-smelling coffee, but no cream. Instead, before she even tried to help herself, the waiter poured equal amounts of coffee and hot milk into her cup, from two jugs simultaneously. Café au lait, Carol Anne realized, French-style. She'd never tried it before. Odd that a French style should be found in Jamaica. But perhaps it was a local style, too. This too would have to go down in a note to Mr. Roxlet.

After breakfast, since nobody seemed to expect anything of her, Carol Anne decided to stroll around the hotel grounds to see what could be seen. She'd put on a lightweight one-piece green dress and had taken the precaution of wearing low-heeled shoes in case she had to do a lot of walking. But so as not to look altogether too workmanlike, she'd carefully knotted a green polka-dot silk scarf around her neck. She had a long, slim neck, and the scarf always accentuated it, wnich of course made her feel gorgeous and desirable, or so she'd told her reflection in the mirror earlier that morning. Afterward she wondered if Robert Innes would notice.

She walked down the creaking steps to the courtyard, but as she reached the last one a pleasant male voice called her name.

"Miss Todd? How are you this morning?"

An elderly mustachiod gentleman with an unusually erect posture was advancing from the side of the house to meet her. He wore a beige cotton shirt and matching slacks, and his left arm was in a sling. As he swept off the

38

battered khaki hat he wore, she saw that though his hair was white it was as thick and as curly as a boy's. He put the hat in his left hand and stretched out the other. Carol Anne smiled in pleasure at the welcome on his face.

"You must be Captain Innes," she said, going toward him to take his outstretched hand. "You look just like Robert."

"Bless you, my dear. Years older of course. Excuse the arm. Damned silly accident, truly. Should have been more careful. My own fault, of course. Be better tomorrow, I'm told. So. You're the young lady who's going to put our hotel on the map. Very pleased to meet you, truly. Did you sleep well? Have a good breakfast? All very new to us, you know, this sort of thing. You'll have to give us pointers. Don't hesitate; just come right out and say what you think. Mean it, truly. Want the exercise to be a success, you know, truly."

Carol Anne laughed in delight. She knew right away that she could talk to this charming old man, could communicate with him. The assignment was going to be easy, now that they'd met. The Captain laughed too, as if sensing the same thing. He took Carol Anne's elbow and led her toward a path leading through the flowering shrubs.

"Start with the grounds, shall we? New swimming pool just being finished off today. Has to be ready for tonight. Party, you see. In your honor."

"Mine?" She stopped, but he urged her on, laughing.

"Naturally, my dear. Sheer coincidence the pool's just been finished. Mandeville crowd want to see it. So what better than a party?"

"Why, naturally," Carol Anne agreed, falling into step, "we must by all means have a party to christen the new pool."

"Mandeville crowd wants to take a look at you too, don't forget."

"I'll be at my shiny best." They both laughed again.

The path led through an ornamental garden, beautifully

39

kept, filled with flowering bushes whose names Carol Anne couldn't even begin to guess, then over a lawn dominated by an enormous spreading mango tree from which the fruit hung heavily, then through another hedge of flowering shrubs and onto a wide flagstoned patio with a fair-sized odd-shaped pool in the middle of it and a cabana bar at one end.

Workmen were cleaning up around the patio. The place smelled of new concrete, and water was only a few inches deep in the pool as yet.

"Cost a fortune. Robert was set to have a fit. Architect fellow from Kingston designed it. Looks inviting, though. Should please our guests? What do you think?"

The setting was delightful, with all the flowering shrubs and hedges around the patio. Carol Anne took it all in.

"Presume we did the right thing, eh? The pool?"

"But of course you did; you have to have a pool, and this one's superb."

"Hoped you'd say so. Robert was dead against it, of course. Said people should ride over the hill to the beach. Can't see it meself. Sharks, you know; nasty things. Bite. Beach is crawling with them. Idea people'd much prefer a pool."

"It seems to me Robert isn't at all happy with the idea of turning the manor house into a hotel."

"You noticed that? Dead set against it. Stubborn as his mother, bless her. Wants to spend all the money on new farm machinery instead. All wrong, of course. Times have changed. Farming isn't what it was. Sugar's dropped through the bottom of the market. Fruit isn't wanted. Terrible business. But we have to change with the times, truly we do. Tourists; that's what we need. Rich Americans and Canadians. Bring their dollars here and spend 'em. Waste of time to buy more machinery. Told the blighter so; won't speak to me now. Terrible business, truly. Silly man doesn't realize it, but the hotel's the only way to save the farms. Hate doing it just as much as he

40

does. But no hotel, no farms. Money, you know. It's as simple as that m'dear."

"How awful." Carol Anne was thinking of the two men no longer speaking to each other, but the Captain took another meaning.

"Tried everything. Even set up a cooperative, some years back, with the other farmers in the district. Fellow named McKinnon heads it. Sells all our produce at best prices, but we still can't make a go of it. He'll be here tonight. So will Cathy. His daughter, you know. Been in Europe for the last two years. Robert used to be sweet on her."

"Oh?"

The Captain's white eyebrows arched high as he peered at Carol Anne, but he didn't comment on the tone of voice with which Carol Anne had said the word "Oh." Even so, she knew he'd noticed it, so she began to blush, and immediately hated herself for it. Why had she let that word slip out in just that way?

"Harrumph," said the Captain, taking Carol Anne's elbow again. He led her around the pool toward the small stone-backed cabana bar. It was open on three sides to the weather, and there were ten or twelve bar stools around the bar, with tables protected by big parasols nearby.

"Let's sit here, my dear, and have something cool." The Captain made sure Carol Anne was comfortable, then turned to the smiling man behind the bar and called out something in the singsong local dialect. Then he sat too, but said nothing, giving Carol Anne time to collect her thoughts.

Cathy McKinnon, Carol Anne was thinking. So there *is* a girlfriend in the background. Hardly to be wondered at, really. But hadn't the Captain said Cathy McKinnon had been away in Europe for the last two years? Had she just got back? Perhaps she was a married woman now. Come to that, she didn't even know if Robert was married. But how could she find out diplomatically?

41

When the drinks arrived, Carol Anne tried a careful question.

"Are there any other guests in the hotel yet?" she asked casually as she sipped her drink

"No, m'dear, you're our only one. So we'll take special care of you. You're our guinea pig. Have to see how you like the place before we open it up officially." The Captain raised his glass in a toast.

"Goodness, that does make me feel important." Carol Anne laughed.

"Oh, but you are. Thoroughly respected agency, your Mr. Roxlet's. Good word from your agency would put us right on the map. Bad word, we're dead. Don't be alarmed, m'dear; we don't expect a glowing recommend. But we don't expect a bad report either, because whatever you don't like, we'll change. Robert and his penny-pinching be damned." He smiled, beaming at her. "Take the pool for one. You like it, eh? So that's already one for our side, right? We're getting along famously, so don't worry about a thing." He raised his hand slightly as if to pat her knee, then caught himself in time and patted his own knee. For a naughty moment Carol Anne wished he'd done what he first intended. She liked this old gentleman. His abrupt manner of speaking couldn't hide the fact that he was very concerned for the success of his pet project, and that it hurt him to have to battle with his son over it. He must feel awfully alone, just like she'd felt last night in that big bed. But perhaps his wife was on his side.

"What docs Mrs. Innes think about the hotel idea?"

"Doesn't think about it. Been dead for years, God rest her."

"Oh, I'm sorry . . ."

"Don't be. Happened more than ten years ago. Thrown by a horse. Would have lived forever otherwise. Charming woman, if a bit headstrong. Robert takes after that side of her. Mandeville girl. We had a good life. Childhood-sweethearts sort of thing. Marvelous woman. Great polo player. Dead now." He frowned, lost in momentary reflection. "Don't think she'd really like the hotel, though."

Heavens, thought Carol Anne. He really is alone. Even his long-dead wife wouldn't like this hotel idea of his. Poor old dear. I'll have to help him.

"Well, I think the idea of making a hotel out of a grand old Jamaican manor house is just perfect," she said confidently. "I'm positive the Innes Estate Hotel will very soon be one of the really 'in' places. Everybody will want to come here, and I'm going to help you all I can to make sure they do."

She got up from her seat. "Now, you simply have to show me the rest of the place; there must be dozens of things I should see." She tugged at his good arm, so he put down his drink and got up too, beaming at her eagerness.

"Tell me, Captain, doesn't anybody think you're doing the right thing? How about the other Mrs. Innes, Robert's wife."

"Ha! There isn't one. But there should be. It's what the fellow needs, a good wife. Keep him from working himself to death. Flogging a dead horse. And for what? Costs more to plant the fields, some years, than we get for what we sell off 'em."

They were taking a different direction, past the other side of the huge mango tree, and up a rise to the peak of the hill on the side of which the manor house was built. Both needed their breath for walking.

They came to the top of the rise. The manor house was on one side, and the far-stretching acres of farmland reached off into the distance on the other.

"Look at it," grumped the Captain, waving his arm at the fields. "Three hundred years and more in the family. Always gave us a good living. More than fifteen hundred acres. You'd think we could clear fifty pounds to the acre, eh? Well, we don't. Haven't for years. Not since m'wife died. Closer to five pounds, some years. Can't run the

43

place on that. Had to sell off land instead." He stared indignantly at the spreading land. Carol Anne shaded her eyes to look where he was looking.

Away in the distance sat a man on horseback, talking to some field hands. Though he was a figure made tiny by distance, she recognized him. The oddest sensation came over her when she did, and she had to catch her breath.

"Isn't that your son, away over there?"

The Captain laughed delightedly. "You've got sharp eyes, m'dear. But then, that's traditional on this spot. Find-your-man Hill, it's called. Generations of Innes women came here. Peeked out over the fields to see what their men were doing. Family tradition. Also tradition to court your girl here. Courted me own dear lady, right on this spot. Many years ago. Far too many. Come. Show you the place I proposed." He stepped off the grassy knoll and indicated a flagstone path leading behind a huge flowering bush.

"Take a look, m'dear. Historic spot. She accepted me, right on that stone bench there, my lady love."

It was an exquisite bower, scented and sheltered, just below the brow of the hill. The bush behind it hid it from anyone on the hilltop, but the view from the stone bench was of the distant fields. There was a tiny green patch of lawn before the bench, with a moss-covered statuette in its center. Flowers twined and interlocked around the bench, while swift hummingbirds foraged for nectar in their blooms.

"Oh, Captain. How lovely! Why, this spot alone could make your hotel famous."

"Like it? Delighted to hear it."

"It's beautiful!"

"Good name, eh? Find-your-man Hill? Two meanings, when you think about it." He chuckled quietly. "My good lady find-her-man here," he added in the local singsong dialect. Carol Anne laughed with him.

"Well. Lots to see yet. Come along, m'dear." But instead of setting out at once, the Captain lingered, searching the far horizon again. Carol Anne looked too, taking in the long symmetrical rows of fruit trees in the distance, the swaying crops in the green fields, the field hands working. It all seemed so efficient and well-cared-for. How could such an enterprise be having money troubles?

"What do you think is the matter with the farms?"

"No mystery at all, m'dear. We grow fine crops. Sugar. That's our mill in the distance. Oranges. Over there behind the village. Peaches too, on the slope behind the manor house. Mangoes, of course. Akee. Even rice in the swampy land behind the sugar mill. All kinds of crops. All good stuff. Good yields, and no wonder; Robert breaks his back from dawn to dusk. But the market's gone sour. Been that way ten years. Economy's all gone to pot. We grow it, sell it, pay taxes and shipping, then hardly a trickle of money comes back to us. That's the mystery; not the land, not the crops, but the market—the money. It just isn't there. Ever since my good lady left me. Shot the horse, by the way. Magnificent animal, but can't have that sort of thing. Shot him myself." He took off his hat and fanned himself with it for a moment.

"But that's enough about our troubles. Must show you the hotel part instead. Lots to see yet, truly." He jammed his hat back on his head and took Carol Anne's elbow, ushering her ahead of him, around the brow of the hill onto the flat land where the house was built. As soon as they reached it, a cool breeze greeted them, ruffling her hair. She shook it free, glad that she'd washed it last night.

The level land around the house encompassed about ten acres in a rough rectangle dominated at one end by the manor house itself, and at the other by the peak called Find-your-man Hill. There were tennis courts on the grounds, well-kept clay courts which the Captain showed her. "Me dear lady had them built, long ago," he informed her proudly. Just past the courts was a stretch of billiard-table-green cropped lawn in an exactly accurate rectangle, bordered by a shallow inches-wide gravel ditch,

45

with red barberry hedges behind it. "Croquet," he announced. "Old-fashioned game, but people who play it get to like it." There was a very young boy on the lawn picking out weeds on his hands and knees. The Captain greeted him by name, patting his rump in passing.

"Come. More to see," he said, urging her on.

He marched her behind the manor house, where there was a row of old stone-built stables. "Riding. Good for the liver. Best exercise there is." He would have moved on, but Carol Anne insisted on going inside the sweet-smelling stables to pet the velvet noses and smooth the muscular necks. He had to promise she could go riding next morning before she would leave.

"Good idea," he agreed. "Get Robert to show you the place where we're laying out the golf course. Ride over to the sugar mill too, if you like; smelly place, but visitors always find it amusing. I won't go along. Not as young as I was, eh?" He looked at his watch. "Time for lunch very soon. Perhaps you'd like to call a halt for now? After lunch you might want to swim in the pool; you'd be the first—sort of christen it. Plan to take a siesta myself. Usually do, right?"

He escorted Carol Anne back to the wide front steps of the manor house, leaving her there with a flourish of his khaki hat and a smiling bow.

"I'll see you at lunch, then, right? In about half an hour, shall we say?"

Upstairs in her room Carol Anne discovered that the giant bed didn't look at all menacing any longer. It looked really welcoming. She flopped onto the coverlet on her back, gasping. It had been an energetic morning. But on sudden impulse she kicked off her shoes and stood on the bed, reaching up for the canopy. She tugged gently, then harder, finally really hard, then breathed a sigh of relief. That canopy wasn't about to come down. It was as firmly in place as if nailed there. Well, one less thing to worry about. But she felt a tiny bit embarrassed as she flopped back on the bed again. How silly to be scared of a canopy.

46

From the corner of her eyes, lying on the bed, she saw her lavender dress carefully laid over a chair back. She sat up.

Someone, probably the maid, had washed and ironed it. She picked up the dress. Not only that, but they'd starched it. Dubiously she fingered the suddenly stiff material, wondering how it would feel when she got it on. Then she saw that all her things had been washed; everything she'd used so far, even the white nightgown with the pink bows. It was fluttering on a hanger by the window, as was her wine-colored underwear at another window. She turned bright pink and hastily took everything down, folding the clothes and putting them away, but at the same time making a mental note to find out precisely what the laundry facilities were in the planned hotel.

She looked in the drawer where she'd put her papers, and found the two-page form Mr. Roxlet had given her, on which she was to check off her estimate of the services and facilities available at the hotel. She found the place where it mentioned "swimming pool" and ticked it off. Also tennis courts and stables, hesitating over golf course, then deciding to wait until she'd actually seen it in the morning. But she couldn't find a place to check off a croquet lawn that looked like a giant billiard table, nor anywhere at all where she could describe the beauty of Find-your-man Hill with just a check mark.

So she found a sheet of notepaper, sat down and in a moment was scribbling furiously, trying to explain these wonders in her own words. She filled two pages with her enthusiasm before she was sure Mr. Roxlet would understand how gorgeous this place was now, and how entrancing its future visitors would find it. Then she remembered promising to meet the Captain for lunch, and hurried into her bathroom to freshen up.

Chapter Four

Dressed in white and filled with glee at the thought of seeing the charming old Captain at lunch, Carol Anne flew out of her room and was about to skip rapidly down the stairs when she had a sudden thought. She hadn't yet discovered how many rooms there were in the manor house.

So, anxious to get downstairs, she hurried along the corridor, counting the doors. It shocked her. So that when at last she was downstairs, hurrying out to the veranda where lunch as well as breakfast were to be served, she was already blurting out her surprise.

"There are only twenty rooms!"

Then she stopped dead. The Captain wasn't there, but Robert was, dressed in khaki jodhpurs and a white shirt, his tanned arms contrasting sharply with the crisp whiteness of his shirt. Color mounted to her cheeks. He stood there, leaning possessively against the veranda rail, a drink in one hand, looking every inch the owner of this house, making her feel suddenly a stranger. Was she wrong, or had he been smiling when she burst through the door? But he certainly wasn't smiling now.

"That's right," he said in his deep voice, "precisely twenty."

She came slowly forward, her chin held high. "But

twenty rooms would never be enough to make the hotel pay," she argued. "You'll need at least double that number." Then she smiled. "But if they're all as big as my room, it would be simple to partition them and turn them into two rooms each."

"No." Robert's voice was stern. Carol Anne's smile faded away and she stopped. But just then they heard footsteps coming up the wooden steps leading from the grounds, and they both looked. The Captain was arriving, dressed in a light beige linen suit, wearing a pleased smile the moment he saw Carol Anne. Then he saw Robert leaning on the rail, and the smile became touched with concern. "Hello, Robert. Come home, have you? Nothing wrong on the farms?"

"I've got everything done that can be done today, so I thought I'd take a break."

The Captain's smile grew wide again. He turned to Carol Anne. "You're looking charming, m'dear. Charming. That's a pretty dress. Shall we take a table? See if the luncheon crew knows their duties, eh?" Then he turned to Robert again. "Join us? Do you good to have a civilized meal for once instead of whatever it is you manage to snatch a bite of down below." He pulled back a chair for Carol Anne, then took the one to her right. Robert put his drink on the table to her left before sitting down.

"What have you two young people been arguing about?"

The Captain's question was so abrupt and to the point that Carol Anne was caught by surprise at his perspicacity. She answered unthinkingly. "I've just discovered there are only twenty rooms in the manor house. That just isn't enough to make the hotel pay. You'll need at least twice that number."

"And she wants to cut them up into two smaller rooms each," added Robert in a grim voice that dared his father to take her side. She glanced at him. She was very aware of him next to her; of the rather pleasant horsey odor that rose from his clothes; of a sort of warmth that came to her

49

from him. It all made her feel small and vulnerable, but at the same time somehow protected. The combination of strange feelings added up to an overall sense of weakness, of being willing to please. But at the same time her professional pride insisted she fight off this feeling. It simply wouldn't do to let him get away with having his father open the hotel containing only twenty rooms. It would invite swift failure.

But it was the Captain who rescued her. He had just picked up the menu and was about to study it when Robert spoke. Now he put it down so quickly it made a slight noise. "Hah!" he barked. "Didn't that architect fellow say the same thing?"

"And I'm giving the same answer, Father. I'd rather die than see the manor-house rooms cut up into cubicles for strangers."

It was immediately evident to Carol Anne that she had accidentally opened up an old argument between father and son. She kept the words she was about to utter in her mouth.

"Architect says it. Miss Carol Anne here says it. Got to cut up those rooms or the hotel's a bust. Can't you listen to reason?" The Captain's white eyebrows were bunching as he glared at Robert.

"You'll just have to charge more. But the rooms can't be changed." Robert's own black brows were bunching too, now. The two of them looked like an older and a younger version of the same man. And though instinctively Carol Anne's heart sided with the younger, it did so by trying to point out to him what was for his own good. Sensible, feminine logic, which no man could be expected to understand.

"But without enough rooms, you can't even open!" Her eyes were wide. "Surely you have to do whatever is necessary to open, now that you've gone this far."

The Captain glared at his son, daring him to refute this common sense. But said nothing. Robert took a deep breath and held it, on seeing this, Carol Anne realized

50

she was holding her own. She let it out in a sigh, then forced a smile on her face.

"I'm hungry," she said diplomatically. "All that walking around in the fresh air did my appetite wonders."

The men took the hint and dropped the subject. But Carol Anne knew it was only for the time being. It simply had to be brought up again, because it was a huge problem and needed to be solved.

They ate in the harmless atmosphere of small talk, asking each other polite questions, pretending to be absorbed in the answers, but each was aware that under the superficiality of the conversation brooded an explosive pool of contention. So though Carol Anne had been silently luxuriating in the feel of the presence of Robert at her side, it was almost with relief that she saw him put down his napkin after having had only some soup and a sandwich, and rise to his feet. She looked at him.

"I have to get back down to the farms," he said, with his eyes only on her, as if it didn't matter if his father knew where he might be going, but he wanted Carol Anne to know. "They're getting the cane ready for firing, and I want to supervise it." He smiled briefly and left, striding down the veranda steps and off toward the stables. She watched him go, feeling a sense of loss. He wore tiny spurs, she noticed, on the heels of his boots. They jingled merrily as he strode over the cobblestones.

"Excellent," said the Captain with a note of triumph in his voice. "Now we can talk in peace." Surprised at his manner, she shifted her gaze to him, but while his voice had sounded triumphant, his face looked sad. Poor old man, he must really be torn between his problems and his concern for his son.

"This business of the rooms," the Captain continued. "I've known about it too, you see. Very much on my mind. Problem, of course, but problems are to be solved, right?"

He talked, she listened, offering advice, and they continued their meal, and though she somehow missed the

51

brooding presence of Robert at the table with them, it really was a relief to be able to get down to important matters without the fear that his angry outbursts would interrupt. Robert didn't fade all the way out of her mind, but he politely took a quiet spot in the back of it, and waited while she and the Captain worked.

Two hours later Carol Anne came into her room, found the form Mr. Roxlet had given her, slowly clambered up onto the bed, kicking off her shoes as she did, and with an unladylike grunt seated herself cross-legged in the center of the coverlet. She looked for the item asking for her comments on dining-room service, taking her time, blinking drowsily as she did. She just couldn't move any faster if her life depended on it; never in her life had she eaten such an enormous, delicious lunch. She was full to the eyebrows.

"Ah, here it is," she murmured audibly, the pencil at her lips. The category squares were graded from bad to excellent. She tapped the pencil against her teeth.

Then she slowly wrote "Superb" across all the category squares and fell back exhausted on the bed, dropping the pencil and the form.

The sun was much lower in the sky when she awoke, hours later. It was shining on the back of the house, leaving her room in shadow. She felt marvelous, and stretched languorously, flexing every muscle, reveling in the luxury of it. No wonder the Captain takes a nap after lunch every day; everybody should, it's so delicious.

But when she stood up and stretched, she felt grubby. She'd slipped on a white sharkskin dress with a square neck and no sleeves to go down to lunch, and now it was all wrinkled and creased. She unzipped and stepped out of it, thought for a moment, then rummaged in a drawer and found her swimsuit, a one-piece in blue with a large flower pattern. She held it up, wondering if it would still fit after that enormous lunch, then peeled down to nothing, determined to give it a whirl and find out. She stood in front of the mirror smoothing the swimsuit against her. It fit like a second skin. What a pity there was nobody here to see her in it. Robert, for instance.

She posed, one hand on hip and the other held up with a drooping hand on the end, her hip provocatively out-thrust, smiling superciliously at her reflection. How does that strike you, Robert? Then she laughed at herself, grabbed up her terry-cloth robe and hurried off for the pool, looking forward to a nice refreshing dip with nobody around. And maybe a little midwinter suntanning afterward. Such luxury!

She arrived at the break in the hedge just as Robert Innes was standing at the edge of the diving board. He was brown all over, she realized with a start. And far from being the least bit flabby, he was all smoothly rounded muscles, flexing and rippling as he bounced on the end of the board. His pose was unaffected. He obviously hadn't expected anyone else to be at the poolside to see him. She stopped. He'd seen her, so it was too late to turn back. A frown seemed to pass across his face as if he was annoyed at her intrusion. Without a word he arced off the board in a fast, toe-touching dive and entered the water with hardly a splash.

Undecided whether to go or stay, she stood watching him swim the length of the pool in a furiously noisy crawl, turning end-over-end in the shallows and splashing energetically back. With a toss of her head she walked around the pool, found a deck chair, and spread her towel over it before she lay down.

She watched him swim six lengths nonstop. Finally Robert climbed the steps, breathing heavily, and came over, flopping into the creaking deck chair next to hers. He grunted as he lay back, not acknowledging her presence with any greeting.

She didn't say anything either. Oddly, she couldn't think of anything *to* say. But she was very aware of his presence. She reached into the pocket of her bathrobe and found her sunglasses. They had extra-dark lenses; she'd

53

bought them especially for this trip. She felt more secure when she had them on, as if she could hide behind them and not be seen.

The silence lengthened. Robert's breathing was more even now, and not so noisy. She made a distinct effort not to look at him, but eventually she couldn't resist taking a peek. She saw him propped up on one elbow appraising her, and at once she felt a wave of color washing over her untanned skin; her swimsuit suddenly felt much too skimpy. She wished she'd kept her bathrobe on instead of hanging it over the chair. Next to Robert Innes' bronzed body her own winter-pale complexion looked positively naked.

He sat up and started to wipe the water droplets from his arms. "You should always dry yourself after swimming in the tropics," he told her. "If you don't, every drop of water acts like a tiny little magnifying glass and you'll get little sunburn blisters."

"I never knew that." She got up and handed him the towel she'd been lying on. "Here, use this," she said shyly. He took it and got up too, toweling himself vigorously while she lay back on the deck chair and watched him, smiling at his display of energy while her uneasiness slowly evaporated.

His hair was as thick and curly as his father's, but a glossy black. Now that they'd just been dried, the curls were wildly awry; there was something untamed in the sight. His head and neck and his forearms to above the elbows were burned darker than the rest of him, probably from being out in the fields all day, but he'd managed somehow to acquire a smoothly even tan over the rest of his body, making him appear magnificently healthy.

The sun must be awfully hot, because she was feeling very warm indeed. Should she roll over and let the sun at her back? But she'd hardly been here—surely she couldn't be so tanned already. Nevertheless, she felt as if she was baking. And she had never been so aware of anybody in her life as she was aware of Robert creaking down into the deck chair next to hers. Even though she couldn't see him she could sense every move he made. Now he was lying back, wriggling himself into a more comfortable position on the chair, making it squeak again. She felt so tense that she would simply have to get to her feet and run, or swim, or do something physically exhausting soon or die. But she didn't want to leave her place next to Robert.

She chanced another surreptitious peek at him.

He was propped up on one elbow again, boldly looking at her.

The color mounted again, all over her—she was sure she must be as pink as a salmon. She tried to outstare him. So he smiled, a confident, possessive sort of smile which made her furious so that she glared at him wide-eyed. He laughed lightly at her expression.

"You're pink and rosy all the way from your toes to your nose," he informed her, still laughing.

"Nice people are brought up to believe it's rude to stare." It infuriated her to notice that, even to herself, her voice sounded petulant when she said it. She deliberately looked away from him, staring up into the sky.

"But I like pink skin. Around here all I ever see are tanned or brown skins. But that's odd? Surely a travel agent like you would be tanned too? I mean, you must hop from one glamour spot to another I suppose; don't you ever take time out for a little sunbathing at these places?"

He was making fun of her. She was sure of it. Had he guessed that this was her first assignment? Was he trying to provoke her into admitting it? She hadn't heard his deck chair squeak, so evidently he hadn't moved; he must still be staring at her. It made her feel strangely excited, and the feeling showed through in her voice when she answered him.

"You'd better not stare like that at your hotel guests when they start staying here. You'll frighten them away."

She heard his chair squeak. She sensed that he was leaning closer to her. Her eyes were irresistibly drawn toward his; her face turned too, though she hadn't willed

55

it. His own face was close to hers—she noticed his lips at once. They were a deeper red than they had been. She kept her eyes on them while he spoke in a voice that was only partly teasing; it also sounded as if he was speaking something he believed was true.

"None of them will be worth looking at, now."

And then he kissed her on the mouth. And while it lasted she lay perfectly still, unable even to think. The whole world was still for that moment; a little sliver of eternity until he leaned back, making his deck chair squeak again.

Her first impulse was to leap to her feet and run, but she controlled it, shocked by the fact that another impulse, almost as swift as the first, had tried to make her kiss him back. So for a moment she lay there with wildly contrasting thoughts running through her head before suddenly she leaped to her feet, took two swift steps and dived into the safety of the pool.

Oh, how cool and refreshing it was! How pleasantly safe and secure to be five or six feet down in these cool green depths, millions of miles away from Robert Innes and his calmly confident masculinity.

She swam underwater as long as her breath held out, reaching the other side, turning underwater toward the deeper end, diving even lower before, gasping, she shot for the surface and emerged with a great splash and splatter, thrashing wildly while she took deep breaths.

She was no longer unbearably hot. She didn't even look at Robert. Instead, having read somewhere that nature in her mysterious wisdom had made women as a group better swimmers than men as a group, she set out at a fast crawl for the shallow end. And when she got there she dived and turned underwater and headed strongly back toward the deep end, working off the explosively abundant energy with which she had somehow become filled within the last few minutes. But at the same time she knew Robert was watching her, and she wanted him to know that she was an excellent swimmer. And, she gleefully admitted to herself, to get a good long look at herself in her new swimsuit if that was what turned him on. She blushed again as she swam, the thought reminding her of his kiss.

Why had he kissed her?

Was it just a sudden male impulse? Did he already regret it? Worse, did he think she was silly to have jumped into the pool right after he'd done so—like a frightened schoolgirl? She was suddenly furious with herself. She swam as strongly as she could, trying to dissipate the feeling, making so much splashing and noise that she didn't hear Robert dive into the pool. The first she knew of it was when, as she lifted her face for a breath, she saw him swimming effortlessly alongside her, his pace easily matching her own, even though she redoubled her efforts the moment she saw him, trying to go faster. He smiled when he caught her eye, but it wasn't a competitive smile, just a companionable one; he wasn't even thinking of racing her! He was so confident he was the better swimmer that he was just lazing along, with not a thought in his mind that her pace should be making it difficult for him to keep up.

She rapidly tired of the sport when she realized he had already won the game without trying, so she swam to the steps and climbed out. He followed right behind her, and she knew his eyes were on her; she could almost feel them appraising her. Did he look his horses over like this before he rode them? She had to walk to her chair in her most erect and careful manner, knowing that he was watching her, and praying that her hips wouldn't swing. She had an almost uncontrollable desire to swing her hips just to hear what he'd say, and it made her laugh, so that by the time they were toweling themselves dry they were both laughing, though neither knew why. But the laughter had melted whatever iceberg had existed in the atmosphere earlier. When they sat down in their deck chairs again it was without any awkward politeness, as it had been earlier, and instinctively Carol Anne was aware that she had to pretend the kiss had never happened.

She wanted to talk to him. What would he be interested in?

"The Captain tells me a friend of yours has arrived back from Europe. A girl named McKinnon."

He looked surprised. Then he grinned as he tossed the towel over the chair back and lay down again. "Cathy McKinnon, eh? I didn't know she was back in these parts."

Carol Anne felt an unreasonable surge of jealousy and tried at once to smother it. What right had she to feel jealous? Or anything else, for that matter?

"So Cathy's back, eh?" he rubbed his hands together and grinned up at the sky. "Hmmmm."

Well! The man needn't show such delight at the news, Carol Anne thought furiously. He was acting like a boy on his birthday morning; couldn't wait to get his hands on the presents.

"Your father's letting me go riding in the morning," she said at last. "He says I should see where the golf course is being laid out."

"Damned silly waste of land." Robert's smile vanished momentarily, and Carol Anne promptly felt better. But his smile reappeared when he turned to talk to her. "So you ride, eh? I thought you were a city girl. Do you shoot, too?"

"Shoot?" Visions of guns and noise. "No, I don't think so." Then a nasty suspicion entered her mind. "I'll bet Cathy McKinnon does, though."

"Oh, Cathy? Of course. An excellent shot. Eyes like an eagle. But you don't shoot, eh?" He sounded surprised, peering at her as if trying to see her eyes through the dark sunglasses. She felt an urge to stick her tongue out at him.

"I'm not saying I don't. It's just that I never have, so I don't know if I do or not."

He rolled back to stare at the sky again, and once more

he grinned and rubbed his hands together. The hound! She decided to get his mind onto something else.

"I saw you today, out in the fields on a horse—"

"Father took you to Find-your-man Hill, eh?" He interrupted. "It's a great view from there; you can see nearly all the farms."

He frowned, locking his fingers together and laying them on his stomach. For a few moments he was silent; then, "Everything's going so well this year," he said at last. "No hail, no blight, plenty of rain; it looks like it will be a good year."

"Then why are you frowning?"

"Am I?" He grinned self-consciously. "Worry, I suppose. We had a good year last year too, but it doesn't seem to show in the books—but you don't want to hear my problems."

"I don't mind."

"Well, I'll keep them to myself anyway. Your worry is the Captain's hotel. The farms are my problem, and I'll handle it myself." His voice was brusque, almost cutting. Carol Anne withdrew into herself at the sound of it.

What was there that she could talk to Robert about? He was short and to the point about the farms, and he didn't care for his father's hotel scheme. But she didn't want to sit here in total silence; she felt he might get bored and leave if she did. But what else did they have in common?

Cathy McKinnon, that's what, she realized gloomily.

She decided to gamble on being silent. But as the silence lengthened, she remembered something the Captain had told her this morning. She tried to recollect what it was.

"Isn't Cathy McKinnon's father managing a co-op of some kind for the farms around here?" she asked at last. If she had to talk about this Cathy creature, at least let's keep it on the level of her relatives, she reasoned.

"Yes. Douglas McKinnon's our manager. He set up the farm co-op a few years ago when prices started to skid. We did well for a year or two, but even he couldn't hold the line forever. Doug's hardly any better off than the rest of us, even if he is the manager."

"Was he the one who bought your land when you sold off a piece?" she guessed.

"Yes. Seventy acres next to his own land. Our two properties are adjoining, and it made sense in a way, as well as being handy cash when we needed it."

"It sounds to me," she said carefully, "as if he's doing considerably better, if he can afford to buy land from people."

"He got a mortgage from a bank, just as I would have had to if I'd wanted to buy land. Old Doug's a gambler; he believes in this land, just as I do, and he's only waiting for the commodities market to sort itself out, just like the rest of us are."

"Has he bought land from anybody else?"

Robert sat up and stared at Carol Anne.

"I was only wondering," she said defensively.

For some reason she knew she had touched a sensitive area. Robert's jaw tightened and a vein in his right temple visibly throbbed.

"I'm not suggesting there's anything wrong."

"Well," he frowned, "what are you suggesting?"

"Nothing, really. Nothing at all. I was just trying to talk to you about something you might think was interesting."

Just as quickly as his moodiness had come, it vanished. He laughed aloud. "I'm sorry," he said at last. "You must think I'm a real grouch. I hope I'm not. But this farming business is such a ticklish one right now that I suppose I'm allowing it to monopolize my thoughts. Forgive me, will you?"

She smiled at him in answer.

"Tell you what," he said at once. "Go ahead and ask me whatever you want, and I promise not to snap at you." He lay back on the deck chair again, clasping his hands on his stomach.

Carol Anne thought for a while. There were so many things she'd love to know. What was his favorite color, what did he like best to eat? What did he look like all dressed up? So far she'd only seen him in jodhpurs shorts and a swimsuit.

But she couldn't ask him any of these questions. So she turned her mind back to the farming problems which seemed to engross him so much. And once again the thought of one farmer being able to buy land, while the other farmers in his group were doing so badly they had to sell land, came into her mind. It just didn't make sense.

But that, too, was a topic that might upset him. A tiny wave of frustration washed over her: Mr. Robert Innes, she said inside herself, you're such a *touchy* person.

Reluctantly she decided to stick to the one subject that she had learned pleased Robert to talk about. Inwardly she groaned as she asked the next question. The things I'll do to be charming, she told herself, feeling very heroic.

"What has Cathy been doing in Europe? Studying?"

"For a while, so I hear. She took postgraduate work in Rome. Italian studies or something, to round off her degree."

"She has a degree?" Carol Anne prompted, thinking of her own high-school business diploma, which had seemed so important when she got it.

"In medieval history, yes. And an M.A. in Renaissance Italy."

"That does sound impressive. Is she planning to teach?"

"Cathy?" He laughed. "Heavens no. Cathy likes fun too much to waste her time on a lot of grubby schoolkids. No, I don't know what Cathy plans to do."

"Maybe she'll tell you when she comes tonight."

"That's true. I'm looking forward to seeing Cathy again. We had a lot of fun together, for a while. She and I took the mixed-doubles cup three years in a row at the club in Mandeville, so we got to keep it. It's in the manor house now, somewhere."

The sun was much lower on the horizon now, seeming to grow larger as it dropped, turning redder and staining the scattered clouds with a glorious mixture of colors. Robert glanced at it.

"Close to six o'clock," he said with a farmer's confidence in his judgment of time by the sun. "Dinner will be early tonight, because of the party. We should go and get changed."

But he made no move to get out of his deck chair. Surprised, Carol Anne realized that he was enjoying this relaxing moment with her, and was subconsciously prolonging it. It was nice to know that if she hadn't been there with him, he would have probably left for his room as soon as he'd finished.

But he was right. They should go and get changed. So she stood up and gathered her belongings. His deck chair creaked as he got to his feet. Neither said anything as they fell into step and left the pool. But when they were walking along the flagstoned path, Robert spoke.

"You may even have met Cathy yourself, on your travels," he said. "From what I hear, she was forever gadding about Europe—Paris, Rome, London, Zurich—all the fun spots. Cathy is an enormously attractive girl and is forever getting her picture in the papers. Did you ever notice her in them?"

Oh, heavens, thought Carol Anne. Of course he'd imagine that, as a travel agent, I'd have been to all those places.

"I don't know what she looks like, so how could I notice her?" she said evasively.

"Tall girl, very blond. Very clear skin and a classic face. She was beautiful before she left, and the pictures I've seen since she's been away show she hasn't lost it."

She wouldn't have, thought Carol Anne.

Aloud she said, "No, I can't remember seeing her picture."

"Ah, well, you'll see her in person tonight."

"I'm looking forward to it."

Oh no I'm not, thought Carol Anne, smiling at Robert with gritted teeth.

Chapter Five

The maid who was so shy was in Carol Anne's room when she got there.

"The Captain tell me to tell you dinner be early tonight, on account of the party," she informed Carol Anne gravely, as if she had been waiting hours to say it.

"Thank you. I'll be ready."

"Oh, no need to hurry. The men will wait." And unaccountably she giggled. "The men always wait," she added seriously, "when the lady is pretty like you. I remember how they wait when I was a young girl."

Pretty? Carol Anne was pleased. She'd never thought of herself as pretty. Her hair was beautiful, and she was very proud of it. She knew she dressed well—she'd acquired a good wardrobe over the years—and she was by no means ashamed of her looks. But she knew she wasn't outstanding, which was why she'd learned how to be sympathetic and understanding, as a counterbalance. But pretty? She went over to one of the mirrors on the front of an armoire and inspected her face for a second. Nope. Same old me, she told herself. Even so, it was nice to hear what the maid had said.

"Tell me, what's your name?" she asked her. It was silly to think of this woman as "the maid" if she was going to be around here for a week.

"Charlene, miss, and I got four children, and I married, too," she said proudly.

Charlene was holding up Carol Anne's blue sheath dress.

"I look in the cupboard and I find this one, so I press it for you to wear to the party tonight," she announced. "And I pick out these shoes and I put some pretty underthings on the bed. You a lucky lady to have so many pretties."

Carol Anne laughed. "That's exactly what I was planning to wear," she told her, taking the dress and holding it up. "You've done a lovely job of ironing. I was so afraid it would be all creased from being in my suitcase."

"Now I start the bathwater for you," said Charlene, opening the bathroom door. She disappeared inside, and in a moment Carol Anne heard the taps going. How strange, she thought, as she gently laid the dress on the bed next to her underclothes, how luxurious and strange, yet how nice and cozy it was as well to have a personal maid. Somewhere in the world there were people who took such a thing for granted—probably Cathy McKinnon was one of them—but for me, Carol Anne Todd, this luxury will end in a few more days. Ah, well, enjoy it while you have it, girl.

Charlene came out of the bathroom and helped Carol Anne off with her bathrobe. Carol Anne felt like purring as she went into the bathroom and closed the door. She dropped her swimsuit on the floor from an outstretched hand, sure that Charlene would pick it up and wash it. But immediately she rebuked herself and bent down to pick it up, hanging it on the hook behind the door. You're a fraud, Carol Anne Todd, just you remember that, she admonished herself. You don't *have* a personal maid; somebody's only *lent* you one.

But wouldn't it be nice if it could last a little bit longer. The word "forever" passed through her mind, and she inspected it momentarily before regretfully trading it in for "a little longer." This was really only a dream. She counted up the hours in her mind. Just over thirty-six hours ago she had trembled into the airport building in Toronto, icy from the cold, her fingers so stiff that it was painful letting go of her suitcase handles when she got to the ticket counter.

She lifted a hand out of the foamy bathwater and inspected it, flexing the fingers. Somehow, she just couldn't remember what it felt like to be cold. She felt instead as if she'd been here in the manor house all her life, and had only dreamed the part of her life that came before yesterday.

"Aaah me," she sighed, letting herself slide down into the foam until only her head was above it.

She inspected her knees, which were also out of the foam. I wonder if he thought I had nice knees, she mused. I know I've got good legs. Taken altogether, they're good legs. But bit by bit? She raised a foot. Do I have nice feet? She raised the other foot, and began to slide under. "Whoops!" she said aloud, pushing herself back.

What was the Captain's lady like? A Mandeville girl, the Captain had said, so she too would have been used to having a personal maid. I wonder what she did with her days? The Captain had mentioned polo. But nobody can play polo all day, every day. What else would she have done?

Well, there's this great big house to look after. Even with maids and cooks and things, that would take up a lot of time. And then there are the grounds; all those flowers and shrubs. I suppose that was her responsibility, too.

But there would have been plenty of people to do the actual work. All she would have had to do was organize and supervise things. Let me see now, plant that shrub right there. Hmmm. No. Dig it up and move it over a few feet. Carol Anne giggled softly, imagining a handsome, rather arrogant woman giving commands to an army of servants.

But who was to say that she was handsome or arrogant? She could have even been a mousy little woman.

Robert's mother. If she was the Captain's lady, then she was also Robert's mother. Carol Anne felt a sense of loss; she would like to have met Robert's mother.

She could hear Charlene bustling around in the bedroom. What could she be doing? But then she realized that Charlene was making some noise so that Carol Anne would realize time was moving on.

With a sigh, Carol Anne sat up and began to soap herself.

"I take your bathing costume and I wash it," said Charlene when Carol Anne came out of the bathroom.

"It's behind the door."

"You like the new pool? I see Mr. Robert go up there just before you go up. He a nice man, that Mr. Robert, and you a nice lady. You look good together."

"Oh, shush now," said Carol Anne gently.

Charlene giggled. "I tell the truth," she insisted, "you look good together."

"What kind of way is that to talk? What would Mr. Robert say if he heard you?" Carol Anne smiled.

"He no hear me. Unlessing you tell him," and Charlene burst into another fit of giggles. "Anyways, he only come here to eat, so he only hear what said in the dining room."

"Only to eat? Where does he live, then?" Robert had walked her right to the steps of the manor house, but had left her there. She had presumed he meant to go around the back of the house to his own room, somewhere.

"He have a nice cottage which he make the workmen build for him. Small cottage, but very pretty inside. Got everything inside that cottage. Got bedroom and bathroom, all pretty. Only thing hasn't got is kitchen, because Mr. Robert he like to eat here with the Captain."

"So who lives here, then, in the manor house?" Carol Anne had got into her underthings and was slipping into her freshly ironed dress.

"Only you and the Captain, miss." Charlene sighed. "It

not like the old times, when the Captain's lady was alive. Was so nice in the old times. Sooo nice." She sighed heavily, shaking her head. "After she fell from the horse was all change. For long time the upstairs was all closed off. Doors locked. Sheets all over the furniture to keep off the dust. Long, long time. Downstairs too, all sheets over the furniture, excepting one small room in the back near the kitchen where the Captain sleep." Then she beamed a huge smile on Carol Anne. "But now is going be like the old times," she announced. "They'll be people in the house now, because it gone to be a hotel. I like it for to be hotel. Gone be very nice, have people in the house just like when the Captain's lady be living, long time ago."

"Did you know the Captain's lady?"

"Oh, yes miss. I know her. Very nice lady. Everyone so sad when the horse throw her and she killed."

Charlene knelt behind Carol Anne, tugging the dress into a perfect fit while she watched in the mirror. Carol Anne nodded at herself. You'll do, she told her reflection, you'll do. If I can only get the right hairstyle, then, Cathy McKinnon, watch out!

"Now, miss, if you sitting over here, I can do your hair," said Charlene.

"No. Thank you, Charlene. I think I'll do it myself. I want it to be just right tonight."

"Then you not be wanting me anymore?"

"No. Thank you, Charlene. You can go if you want."

"I take the bathing costume with me."

"All right. What time did the Captain say dinner would be?"

"Dinner be when you get there, miss; everybody wait until you get there. The Captain say not to hurry, because they wait in the bar." Charlene left but stood in the doorway looking Carol Anne over before she departed.

"My, you a *pretty* lady tonight, hmm hmm!"

"Bless you, Charlene. And when you get home, tell your husband he's a lucky man."

Charlene left. Carol Anne could hear her giggling all down the hall.

Carol Anne found the bar quite easily, a rectangular room with many soft seats and couches tastefully grouped around low tables. The furniture was modern, she noticed at once. So were the dozens of pictures hung wherever there was space around the walls; dozens and dozens of good reproductions of well-known works, the walls crammed with them, giving an impression of opulence and good taste too. She hesitated at the entrance, not seeing anybody in the room. Its only life was the crackling fire in a huge stone fireplace at its far end. The room itself was aglow with warm, dim light from many gold-shaded lamps. Hesitantly she went in, feeling welcomed by the atmosphere of intimate coziness.

She looked at her reflection in the gold-framed mirror over the mantelpiece. In the room's soft light her eyes were large and dark, and her skin glowed like copper. She moistened her lips and smiled at her image, showing teeth white as pearls in that kind light.

She felt so happy it was like being lightheaded. There was music in her heart; raising her arms, she swirled around in time to the melody within her.

"You make a charming sight, Miss Todd."

She opened her eyes wide, standing perfectly still. Robert stood there, an amused smile on his lips.

"If you dance like that, you'll be a hit with the Mandeville crowd," he added. "At least with the men."

How long had he been standing there? Hot tears stung her eyes in embarrassment. She felt an urge to run off and hide somewhere, but she couldn't escape the mocking way he looked her over.

He came closer, bringing a faint hint of after-shave lotion. She wanted desperately to push him away because she felt trapped, pinned down by his twinkling blue eyes.

"I didn't hear you come in," she said in an uncertain

68

voice. "Is it a habit of yours to spy on people?" She was gathering her wits now, and her resentment was building.

"I would have coughed, but you took my breath away." He took her arm and turned her toward a nearby couch. "May I get you something to drink?"

She nodded. "Something light, please."

As she sank down into the soft couch, Carol Anne felt herself begin to relax. The velvet touch of the cushions soothed her burning shame away. She let her eyes rest on Robert while he gave his order to the politely attentive waiter who appeared when he went to the bar. Robert had his back turned to her. He wore a white dinner jacket which caressed his broad shoulders, falling smoothly in a perfect fit to his narrow, muscular hips. His trousers were dark blue, with a silken, darker blue stripe down the outside seams. When she looked at his gleaming black shoes she smiled; Robert's manservant must have spent an hour achieving that spectacular shine. It was like a black mirror.

Robert brought back the drinks. The glass he put before her was half-filled with fruits and had two straws poking out of it. "We grow most of those fruits on the farms," he said as he sat down beside her on the dark brown velvet cushions.

Carol Anne reached for her glass. The couch, which had seemed so large, suddenly seemed like a love seat, barely wide enough for two. As she picked up her drink, her arm accidentally touched his, and for a moment her heart stopped. The ice cubes in her drink tinkled a warning.

Robert leaned back, casually draping his arm along the back of the couch. She could feel the warmth of his hand near the back of her neck. Oddly, the warmth made her shiver slightly.

"Sorry to keep you waiting, m'dear." It was the Captain, arriving looking flushed and hurried. At once Robert took his arm away and sat up stiffly. She felt him growing cold. There was a definite tension in the air. The Captain seemed to have brought it with him. Father and son were very cool toward one another. Could they have been quarreling again?

The Captain sat on a seat facing her. Carol Anne sought for a topic that would be neutral ground.

"When might the guests be arriving for the party?" she asked. Robert answered, his voice noncommittal.

"The Mandeville crowd are strange people. None of them wants to be first, but they all hate to miss anything. So they could arrive early or late. All you can be sure about is they'll probably all arrive at the same time."

"Except for Cathy McKinnon," added the Captain.

"That's true. Cathy generally times it so that she arrives alone, after everybody else has got there. She makes beautiful entrances, Miss Todd." Robert's voice was mocking her anew, reminding her of his own entrance just now.

"You may call me Carol Anne, if you like." She was looking down at her drink. You can call me anything you want to, anytime you like, and I'll listen, she thought with a sad smile.

And then she considered beautiful entrances. They'd never seemed important before. As she'd descended the wide, sweeping staircase, she'd been aware that she was as well turned out as effort and imagination could make her: the blue sheath dress fitted like a second skin; she'd had to wear a pair of full panties instead of her usual bikini briefs so that their outline wouldn't show. She'd piled her hair up on top of her head and carefully wrapped the ends, then pinned them into a bun. The only jewelry she wore was a pair of pearl-and-gold earrings, half-dollar-sized, and a real gold bracelet on her left wrist. She'd left her watch upstairs. Who needs to know the time at a party?

She decided to practice making entrances someday. If they were good enough for this McKinnon creature, they'd be good enough for her.

Anyway, she promised herself, she'd get these two

talking to each other, even if she had to choose a topic that might make her choke on her drink; Cathy McKinnon.

"So, are you pleased with what you've seen so far?" Carol Anne stared at Robert, still with a smile on her face. Was he trying to be civilized? Or was he thinking she'd say something about the hotel that could give him the chance to argue with his father?

"Delighted," she admitted. "I haven't seen a thing that I can find fault with." Let's see you quarrel with that, she thought.

But Robert actually was trying to be nice.

"I've got to admit the pool is a good idea. We should have had a pool installed years ago, just for our own use. I'm glad to see it there," he allowed, quite graciously.

"And it's in such a perfect setting," she added.

"Architect fellow, from Kingston," supplied the Captain.

"He designed it?" asked Carol Anne.

"Whole thing. Pool, plants, paving. The whole thing."

"He must be very good."

"Did this room."

"So you mentioned. He has very good taste," Carol Anne replied as she looked around.

"Does a lot of things for the hotels on the north shore. Friends of mine up there recommended him. Think it was a good idea? Fellow cost an arm and a leg."

"I think it was a very good idea," she assured him.

"Glad you said that. Robert thinks it was a waste of money." The Captain turned a smile that was mostly glare onto his son. Carol Anne felt a rising tide of panic. So this was what they had been quarreling about. A swift change of subject was imperative. But just then a gong sounded deep within the house.

"Ah. Dinner," announced the Captain happily. He got up from his seat and proffered Carol Anne his arm. "May I escort you, m'dear?" It was only then that she noticed he'd put away the sling from his left arm.

"I'm glad to see your arm's better," she said as she got to her feet. Robert fell in with them, on her other side, and the Captain marched them all into another large room—even larger than the bar—furnished with a dozen tables, each set for six people.

"Goodness. But you already have a dining room outside, on the veranda."

"That's for breakfast and lunch," argued the Captain. "Need a completely separate dining room. More formal. Besides, what about inclement weather? Moths, too. Nighttime they can be a bloody nuisance, hanging about the lamps."

"I said we didn't need it," Robert chipped in. "The veranda setup was perfectly adequate by itself."

"Let me guess," Carol Anne hurriedly interrupted before the Captain could reply. "Architect fellow from Kingston, right?"

"Exactly so. Clever fellow. Sound arguments for this room."

"Well, if this room was a mistake, then it's the first one of his I've seen. So let's not judge it too hastily. After all, you said he'd done a lot of designing for the north-shore hotels, so he must know what he's doing."

"Just what I say. Fellow's highly recommended."

"And highly overpriced, Father."

"Goodness, what a big menu. Can your kitchen really serve all these things?"

"Frozen food, most of it. Swiss company prepackages many of those dishes; all the foreign ones anyway. Architect fellow put me onto them."

"But with all the foodstuffs produced by your own farms . . ."

"Naturally, m'dear. See that row? All local dishes, all fresh produce. Anything at all. Test the cook."

"I . . . I'm really not very hungry. We had such a big lunch." Carol Anne gazed blankly at the long, expensively printed menu. There really was an overwhelming list of dishes, page after page of them. And at the back, an

72

equally long wine list. The menu would certainly have to be changed, she was thinking. It was too intimidating as it was. Something shorter and simpler should be printed, with a reduced list, she mentally noted. Robert saw her studying the menu.

"Shall we have a bottle of wine?" he suggested. "I gave the Captain a hand in stocking the cellar. There's a very good Australian wine there." He touched one of the lines on the list in Carol Anne's hand, accidentally touching her own finger. It was as if an electric shock had passed through her arm.

"By all means let's have a bottle of your Australian wine." She smiled. "Did you really help choose the wines?" Robert nodded, grinning almost shamefacedly. "How nice," Carol Anne said.

But when she looked back at the list, she shook her head. "Seppelt Moyston Australian Claret, 1971?" she asked. "I didn't know the Australians made wine."

"Excellent wine, m'dear. Got to give them credit for it. Give Robert credit, too. For knowing it." The Captain beamed on his son, and for once Robert smiled back. Progress, thought Carol Anne. Now, if we can just keep this up.

"I'll tell you what, Robert. Since you've appeared to do such a great job in choosing the wine, why not also choose what I'll have for dinner? And choose it from the local dishes, from things grown right on the farms." She folded closed her menu.

"Do you trust me?"

Try me, she thought, but only nodded.

"All right then . . ."

"Order for me, too, Robert. Test your skills."

"All right, Father." He leaned back in his chair, studying the menu, while the quietly attentive waiter leaned forward, his pencil poised over a pad. They spoke together in low tones.

While they were discussing the meal, the Captain leaned toward Carol Anne, also speaking in a low voice.

73

"Robert was upset about the architect's bill. Claims we could have done as well without him. Quite wrong, of course. If we're going to have a hotel, it has to be first-class, right? Truly think so, m'self. Blighter believes we should have cut corners to save a few pennies."

Carol Anne patted the Captain's arm in reply, smiling at him. She didn't want to be forced to take sides. She waited till Robert was finished with the waiter before saying anything.

"I've been told you have a cottage on the grounds somewhere. Did you move out because the manor house was being altered?"

"No, no. I've lived in my cottage for years. It always seemed so senseless to keep this huge place open just for two men; armies of maids and servants running about doing nothing but eat. So I had my little place built. I'd have built one for Father, too, but he wouldn't hear of it."

"Of course I wouldn't. Wrong approach entirely, to close up the place. *Open* it up. That's what's needed. Fill it with people. Get some life back in here, the way it used to be."

"In those days the place was filled with family and friends," Robert argued. "You can't equate them with strangers."

"Not strangers, guests," Carol Anne interjected. "Try to think of them as guests." But that only made Robert angry.

"Guests who pay? It's undignified. Strangers sleeping in my mother's room because they can afford to foot the bill? I'll never get used to it." He seized his napkin and unfolded it as if it contained answers to his problems, slapping it on his knees. "But I suppose I will have to get used to it, now that we're committed to this project."

"Right. So try to like it, my boy." The Captain's eyebrows bristled. "We're going ahead, hell or high water. So smile. Give it a good try. Or else stay down in your cottage. Damned right!"

I blew it, Carol Anne groaned. They're at each other's

74

throats and it's because I had to ask a silly question. By sheer luck the waiter appeared at that moment with the wine, and there was a starchy-stiff couple of minutes while he did the business of the wine ceremony, handing Robert the cork to feel, pouring a tiny taste into his glass to see if he liked it. Someone's really trained the Captain's staff, Carol Anne mused. Architect fellow from Kingston? More than likely. I must remember to get his name and address; probably Mr. Roxlet would be glad to know about him.

After the waiter had gone, the Captain returned immediately to the fray. "You may not realize this, Robert, but we *are* committed. The money from the land we sold is spent. It's gone into the hotel scheme. Can't get it back. So work with me. Don't fight me. Can't do any good if you do. Do a hell of a lot of good if you help, instead."

"Father, please . . ." Robert glanced at Carol Anne. But the Captain ignored his hint.

"Miss Todd's no fool. She knows what's happening. Too late to hide anything now. We need Mr. Roxlet's blessing, and she's the only one who can get it for us. So might as well have everything out in the open. Sorry, m'dear, to be so rude. But the matter's important."

The waiter came back with the food. Carol Anne had no idea what she was eating. It might as well have been sawdust. How awful it was that these two nice men should quarrel. And even worse, somehow she felt as if in a way she was the cause of their bitterness toward each other. And it had promised to be such a fun evening, until she'd sensed in the bar what the two of them had been doing.

They ate in silence. And as she ate, it slowly dawned on Carol Anne that she knew exactly what had happened. All the little pieces of the jigsaw puzzle were beginning to fall into place.

She looked at the Captain, busy with his food, then at Robert, eating as if it pained him to. Of course they would quarrel, because Robert simply didn't know the whole

75

story. Perhaps his father was too proud to tell it to him. For if Robert didn't want to see strangers in his mother's house, neither did the Captain. But the older man was willing to have it so, rather than allow any chance of the estate falling into other hands, because the estate was Robert's love. While Robert wanted to save the manor house as well as the farms, the Captain was willing to let the manor house go, just so long as Robert could still have the rest of the land. His plan to turn the manor house into a hotel was intended solely in hopes that, by making enough money, he could save the farms for his son.

She raised her glass of wine. So far she hadn't touched it. And as she did, the words of a formal toast to success tumbled around in her mind. Suddenly the headlights of an approaching car shone through the windows, making patterns on the wall behind her. Then they could all hear the sound of a number of cars arriving.

"That must be the Mandeville crowd," said Robert, folding his napkin, "We'd better be getting over to the pool."

Slowly Carol Anne put down her glass, untasted.

The pool was a translucent aquamarine jewel, floodlit from below. Carol Anne was in heaven, laughing as she clung to the arm of a darkly handsome young Mandeville man who was returning her to her table. She had danced every dance. The Mandeville crowd was turning out be a boisterous, charming, lively group of people filled with boundless energy and a determination to enjoy themselves. Their method seemed to be to make sure everyone around them was having fun, so that they in turn could be happy.

While the Mandeville crowd was of all ages between late teens and early forties, and were of all colors from pure white to at least one tall young man who was deep black, the one thing they seemed to have in common was a sureness, a self-confidence that came from having an established position in their community. Most of them seemed to be landowners and farmers, with a few well-to-do tradesmen as well. They were quite different from the hurried, harried young people Carol Anne knew in Toronto, all desperate to make their way in the world. These people here tonight had already arrived, albeit in a small world of their own. And yet she felt very comfortable among them.

Robert had lost his anger the moment the Mandeville crowd arrived; he'd even offered her his arm as they walked through the fairyland which his workmen had made out of the ornamental gardens dominated by the huge old mango tree. He'd held it out with a smile, and she took hold of it gladly; he walked so fast that it was difficult keeping up in her high-soled shoes. Even with the extra two inches of height they gave her, he still towered over her. But it was nice to be able to hang on to him. She felt she could have lifted both feet and he would have carried her easily, hardly noticing her weight.

The Captain marched close to her left. She took his arm too, and for a moment hugged both arms close.

There were lights everywhere—dim lights of every color, over a hundred of them at least hanging from the mango tree's wide-spreading branches. The moths were in a delirium of joy.

And when they came through the gap in the hedge onto the poolside, they arrived in Paradise. Pretty, flickering colored lanterns everywhere; hanging from swaying bamboo poles, from the branches of shrubs and trees, with candles set inside glass funnels placed on every glass-topped table. The tables were around three sides of the dance floor and the near side of the pool. And within minutes of their arrival the tables were crowded; it was just as Robert had said, the Mandeville crowd all liked to arrive at the same time. There were dozens of happy people to whom the Captain waved and called greetings and who came flocking up at once to be introduced to her.

So many names all at once, so many smiling faces. She still clung to Robert's arm, as if for security. But one young man took her free hand.

"I'm Harry," he told her excitedly, as if it was great news. "And I hate to see the band playing with nobody dancing. So shall we dance?"

Before she could agree or disagree, he was leading her onto the floor. She cast a swift glance at Robert, surprised to catch a fleeting look of disappointment on his face. But in a moment he was following them, a laughing young woman on his arm looking up into his face so that he was forced to smile.

Harry was wrong. Everybody was dancing. The floor was jammed. It was a concrete floor, but the workmen had polished plenty of talcum powder into it so that it was as slippery as ice. But Harry danced divinely. The band was six black men in red-and-yellow blouses with puffed sleeves, energetically buzzing and tapping and blowing into the oddest instruments. The music was pure old Jamaican, with that excitingly strange rhythm people used to call calypso. And the minute they'd finished that number they moved into an up-to-the-minute reggae beat, with one of the band standing to sing completely unintelligible words with a flashing white smile between choruses. The rest of the band chorused with him and after he'd sung he picked up a bamboo whistle and got the wildest notes out of it, dozens of them to the bar, so that the dancers swung their shoulders and waved their hands in ecstacy, and clapped like the converted when he'd finished.

Harry would have monopolized her if he could; they danced two numbers together, but then the other young men began to cut in on him. At first he tried to refuse, with Carol Anne in stitches, laughing at the excuses he gave: "No, she's an awful dancer and will step on your feet," or, "I'd never trust an innocent girl in *your* hands, Richard." She could hardly dance for laughing.

But finally someone cut in, Harry looked at him, but

78

didn't object. With a sigh as lugubrious as could be, he bowed and stepped away. Carol Anne looked to see who it was.

It was Robert. And the music had changed to a slow, sentimental beat. It welled up all around them as he took her gently in his arms. Willingly she let him draw her closer, resting her head just under his chin, molding her body to his, moving with him as if the two of them were one. She felt at peace. Her laughter was gone, but not her joy; that had grown and filled her, and she'd let it, not doing anything to repress the wave of feeling that flowed through her the moment his hands took hold of her. She gave way to it, resting against him, but dancing lightly, tingling with the need to be a feather in his arms. She was in heaven at last. Without realizing it, she sighed.

His right arm slipped farther around her, drawing her closer. She could feel his heart thumping against her cheek. She looked up at his face. He was smiling down on her.

"You look very beautiful tonight," she heard him say. Her own lips parted in a smile. Did he really think so? She nestled back against his shoulder, almost purring. Ah, if only he meant it. But he was probably just being nice. Then she looked up quickly.

"I *feel* beautiful," she told him solemnly. "I feel just marvelous. Maybe it's the Jamaican air." Then she laughed with him.

The music changed. "Tango!" the crowd cried as one. Some girls promptly dragged their partners off the floor, but there were other girls waiting and willing. In no time there were couples dancing and swaying, exaggerating their steps, backs arched and arms held stiffly. Carol Anne couldn't remember having danced a real tango.

But Robert was a master of the dance. He held her tightly, almost lifting her off her feet as he swung her into the intricate steps. She learned them at once because he was so easy to follow, and swung into the movements with

79

as much energy as he himself. People at a nearby table clapped in time to the rhythm. Carol Anne composed her face in what she hoped was an aristocratic Spanish expression, raised her shoulders, and put her heart into the dance. It was thrilling to be held so close by Robert! She could feel every muscle of his body as they swayed and turned, swung and stepped together in time to the heavy beat of the music. She looked up at his face to see if he was as affected by the dance as she was, and caught him laughing in delight, his eyes sparkling in the light of the moon. Her world was complete. She wanted it to go on forever just the way it was now, here in Robert's arms.

But the world rolls on and bands come to the end of even their best numbers, and all too soon it was over. She felt him move away and take her arm to lead her back. But she sensed a reluctance in him when he did it. Did he too feel as she did?

Robert strolled back with her to a table. The Captain was already there. He got to his feet at once, took Carol Anne's hand and led her back to the floor. "Haven't danced since we got here," he complained. "Been waiting till you were free."

She was delighted to discover he was as nimble as she was herself. He matched her movement for movement and step for step in another swift reggae, but as soon as it was over he led her back to the table, claiming he'd not only proved he could still do it, but didn't intend to slip a disk by acting like an old fool. He took his chair and patted her hand when she sat down, then turned to watch the people.

But she wasn't left to sit for more than a moment. Robert was back. "You're fun to dance with." He held out a hand to help her up.

And I'm exhausted, too, she thought. But not too tired to dance with you.

It was the same magic, once they were on the floor. He and she danced together like Fred Astaire and Ginger

Rogers. They *belonged* together; couldn't the big fool see it?

A fast number, and then a heavenly slow one, and then the Mandeville men began to cut in. "Come on, Robert, don't be such a hog." "Let the local lads show what we can do, Robert." "This man must be a bore, monopolizing you like this, miss." And again Carol Anne was in stitches, because Robert's refusals were as dramatic and artful as Harry's had been: "Can't you see she's scared of you?" and "Your feet are too big. If you step on her you'd squash her."

It was Harry who succeeded, but even he couldn't keep her. Man after man cut in, until at last, laughing weakly, she had to claim exhaustion and was led back to her seat, where she sipped a drink the Captain had ordered and tried to get her breath back. Even so, half the Mandeville men wanted to dance with her. They appeared at the side of her chair the moment the band struck up, but she refused them, because Robert had left the floor to sit with her. It was pure delight.

But now a man appeared who didn't want to dance, didn't even want to talk to her in particular.

"Good evening, Captain Innes," he said. "Congratulations on a successful opening night."

"What? Oh, good to see you, Dino. Glad you could come. It *is* going well, isn't it. Carol Anne, like you to meet Dino di Cavour, architect fellow I was telling you about. Dino di Cavour, Miss Carol Anne Todd." The Captain rose to his feet to make the introductions. "You already know Robert, of course."

Dino bowed to Carol Anne in a way that was more graceful than manly. She had the oddest suspicion that she should know him already, from Toronto or somewhere.

"Miss Todd's here on behalf of the Roxlet travel people, the agency you recommended," continued the Captain. Now Carol Anne remembered who Dino di Cavour was.

"Pleased to meet you," she said. "Are you the same

81

Dino di Cavour who designed those hotels in Sicily and Greece? I read about you in our travel trade magazines."

"It's kind of you to remember that." He took a seat next to her, obviously pleased to be recognized.

"But you're an internationally known architect," she exclaimed. "I always thought you had your offices in Paris. The Captain talked about you as if you were somebody local."

"I have an office on the island, of course. Hotels are my business, and Jamaica has many tourist hotels. But I also have offices in Rome, Athens"—he airily waved a long, manicured hand—"and just about everywhere there are hotels which need my skills. I make my rounds and visit them all from time to time."

"But that's simply great. I should have realized." Carol Anne turned to Robert, who so far had done little but glower at Dino. "Mr. di Cavour is one of the cleverest hotel designers in the world. This venture can't fail if he's had anything to do with it. People all over the world want him to do their hotels. Oh, I'm just delighted."

"Only *one* of the cleverest? I thought I was better than that." Dino smiled as he spoke, but Carol Anne felt he really was hurt. She patted his arm. "*The* cleverest," she assured him. "The best there is. You've done a marvelous job here."

"I'm pleased you like it. Shall we dance?"

The band was into a noisy, happy reggae beat. The floor was alive with couples. Carol Anne almost leaped to her feet.

"Why not?" she said, laughing happily.

It really was great to know that the world's best designer had had a hand in renovating the manor house into a hotel. Now that she knew it, Carol Anne permitted herself to realize that, all along, she'd been a little afraid that the Captain might be in over his head, trying to do something about which he really had no clear idea. But now she felt reassured and confident.

Dino danced divinely, but didn't hold her close. He was

a very handsome man, but there was no spark between them, as there was whenever she danced with other men—and especially with Robert. But she had read enough about him in the various trade magazines to know that he was considered to be a complete egomaniac, even a little effeminate, so she understood and didn't mind.

As the music ended she caught a flash of movement at the entrance to the pool area. So did Dino. They both turned to look. The most beautiful woman was standing gracefully there, smilingly surveying the crowd. She wore a loose, flowing white dress and no jewelry at all except for a heavy gold choker. The sleeves of her gown were slit from shoulder to wrist, exposing tanned arms, and the skirt of the dress was also slit, from floor to very nearly waistline, exposing a very charming leg and ankle. Her hair was gleaming blond and loose, cascading over her shoulders like a silken curtain.

"Cathy McKinnon," said Dino in a surprised voice, "I can't seem to go anywhere without meeting her. Will you excuse me? Cathy and I are old friends, so I really must say hello to her."

And with that Dino left her, right in the middle of the dance floor. Cathy McKinnon, now that she'd got the attention of almost everyone there, was coming forward, striding like a man, flashing that charming glimpse of long tanned leg. She and Dino met at poolside, held each other's hands and kissed each other's cheeks like pecking birds. Carol Anne strolled back to her table, her eyes on Cathy McKinnon, her heart slowly settling deep, away down at the bottom of her being. She felt mousy and small; the midnight-blue sheath dress just didn't compare to Cathy's flowing white creation—that dress must have cost a fortune. Even the gold sandals Cathy wore looked expensive. And as for that air of self-assurance Cathy bore? Carol Anne glumly took her seat, and noticed at once that Robert had left the table. She saw him with the crowd around Cathy, greeting her, smiling happily.

"Quite a looker, eh?"

Startled, Carol Anne forgot to be smiling when she looked at the Captain." She certainly is," she admitted.

The Captain laughed aloud. "Well, young lady, you needn't look so glum. You're quite a looker yourself, truly."

"You're just being nice." Nevertheless she smiled.

"Truly. Good as Cathy any day." He slapped his knee for emphasis, nodding his white head.

Dino came wandering back to the table. He looked peeved.

"Cathy always has to be the center of things," he complained. "I never saw anyone so self-centered." He accented some of his words in the oddest manner, puzzling Carol Anne.

"Have you and Cathy known each other long?", she asked.

"Oh, years and years. Everybody knows Cathy, simply everybody. Though I don't know what everyone sees in her. She's quite a charming girl, as long as she gets her own way of course. But then, most women are, I expect." Now he sounded peeved as well.

"Were you and she at the university together?"

"We met at some do in Estoril, the first time. I think it was at the King of Spain's place—the real one, not his son of course. After that it was Rome, Paris, Monaco, simply everywhere. Cathy's the world's worst gadabout, you know." He shrugged his shoulders a lot when he talked, and waved a hand for emphasis. He wore a number of expensive rings.

"Paris, Rome," mused the Captain. "Haven't been there in years. Wartime, when I was there. Must be quite different now. Love to go there again. Must be old hat to you, m'dear, eh? In your job. Travel all the time, I expect."

"Oh, yes, we do a lot of traveling," Carol Anne lied. Well, it isn't really a lie, she argued with herself. Travel agents often have to travel, and I'm a travel agent now. And anyway, I don't want him to think I'm not as good as that Cathy McKinnon. Even so, a small blush crept up her cheeks. She was glad the lighting was dim.

"So, Dino. You think the pool's going to work for us?"

"Why, of course, Captain Innes. It's working already, isn't it? You've attracted the fabulous Cathy McKinnon."

"Cathy?" The Captain laughed. "Local girl. Always comes here. Hasn't for years, perhaps. But always did when she lived in these parts."

"Cathy is a Jamaican? I never knew that. I'd always imagined she was English."

"Her father's a Scot. She herself was born in Uganda, actually. Family left there when that Amin fellow turfed out the Asians. Came here and bought a farm. There's her father now." The Captain waved, beckoning over a tall, angular man with a fringe of red hair over his ears but no hair at all on top. He had a pointed nose and many sun wrinkles around his eyes from squinting into the distance. "Doug?" he called jovially. "Come on over and meet some people."

Doug McKinnon joined them. "Where's your good lady?" the Captain asked.

"She's seated herself over yonder; she'll be expecting me to join her, so I'll not stay long, if you don't mind." Douglas McKinnon smiled bleakly at Dino, then turned a warmer smile on Carol Anne. The Captain made the introductions.

"It's a very pretty party you're throwing, Captain. I would hate to foot the bill for it, however." Doug laughed.

"Oh, come now, Doug. A few bottles of Scotch. A little electricity. What's so very expensive?"

"You've a live band, I see. Couldn't you have done as well with records?" Again Doug McKinnon laughed, but it was a nervous, mirthless laugh. "Times are hard, Captain, and it's the wise man who trims his expenses to match the times."

"Oh, you penny-pinching Scotsmen are all alike. Get away with you and join your lady," and the Captain laughed too as he spoke, but his own mirth was real and hearty. Doug McKinnon took his cue, smiling. He hadn't sat down, but now he bowed very slightly to Carol Anne, froze Dino with a thin smile, and left.

There was a moment of silence after he'd gone. Dino broke it.

"How can that man be that girl's father?" he demanded. "They're as unlike as . . . an ant and a French poodle!" He sounded quite indignant.

"Douglas McKinnon's a good friend," gruffed the Captain warningly.

"Well," said Dino, still in that indignant tone, then sat in silence, sulking.

Carol Anne wasn't really listening. She was watching Robert dance with Cathy McKinnon. They'd danced only with each other from the moment she'd arrived. Once she saw him smilingly refuse to allow one of the Mandeville crowd to cut in. Earlier, when she and Robert had been dancing and the young men wanted to cut in, Robert had let them. But now he was dancing with Cathy.

She sighed, unaware that she'd done so. The Captain's eyebrows rose as he looked at her. He rose to his feet with a groan, acting the part of an old man, making her smile

"I think I'd like to dance," he announced. "Can't sit here like this. People'll think I'm old. Now, who would like to dance with me?"

For a second it seemed as if Dino was actually considering the offer. Carol Anne laughed and rose.

"Delighted," she said, taking the Captain's arm.

And once again it was a mad, gay whirl. Because someone cut in on the Captain almost at once, and others cut in after, and Carol Anne was kept spinning till the very end of the night.

But though she smiled and laughed and talked, she had eyes only for Robert and Cathy, and toward the end, try as she might to discover them, she couldn't see them anywhere. They had slipped away together, into the scented night.

Chapter Six

Carol Anne spent a restless night. No matter how she plumped and punched the pillow, it was never comfortable. Even if a cool breeze did blow through the open window, she felt hot. But if she threw off the covers, it was too cool for sleep. She lay in bed staring up at the canopy, or squeezing her eyes tight-closed and trying to will sleep to come, but to no avail. All she could do—all her mind wanted to do—was torture herself, wondering where Robert and Cathy had gone. Whose suggestion was it that made them slip away from the dance? Carol Anne knew she was feeling nothing but jealousy. Why had Robert kissed her by the pool? Was it because he thought as a world traveler she was used to idle flirtations with the men she met? She cringed at the thought. Well, she wasn't a world traveler, and although the kiss was brief, she knew she had secretly hoped that it meant more to *both* of them.

Fiercely she would snap her mind away from these speculations. What business was it of hers what Robert and Cathy did? Instead, she tried to remember other things. Home. Her mother's house in Cambridge, the house where Carol Anne had grown up. There was a big garden all around it, with a white picket fence that had seemed as high as the sky when Carol Anne was very young, but which was really only four feet tall. In the winters the snow sometimes filled the garden, rising as high as the top of the fence. It was a pretty sight. Robert would love to see it. How would he get along with Mom? If they were to meet, that is. Mom wouldn't understand him. Her idea of a man was someone calm and loving, thoughtful and a happy companion, like her own husband had been. Robert was too abrupt. Too wrapped up in his own problems. Too self-centered; look at the way he had talked about Cathy to her by the pool! No man with a shred of common sense would discuss one woman with another.

Where had they gone? Why had they not come back?

Carol Anne sat up in bed. It was useless to go on thinking like this. She got up and walked to the window, grateful for the cool breeze.

Find-your-man Hill must be over to the right somewhere. Such a beautiful spot. Could they have gone there?

She marched back to bed, determinedly thinking of home again. They'd had a dog when Carol Anne was young, a big black poodle that was forever leaping the fence and running off; a good-natured beast, but without any brains at all when it came to traffic. He'd been run over twice, but he was so big he was never seriously hurt. Just like that donkey on the way up here from the airport; if it had been any smaller, it would surely have been badly hurt, or even killed. And Robert had helped the animal. He was such a good man. Surely Mom would like him. . . .

She didn't know if she'd slept or not, but it was dawn now, coming with a rush, heralded by chirruping birdcalls and a freshening of the breeze. Carol Anne got up at last to stay.

She showered and felt much better, remembering as she bathed that the Captain had promised she could go riding this morning. He'd even promised he'd get Robert to ride with her and show her around the broad estate. But

88

Robert could go hang himself for all Carol Anne cared this morning. She felt worn out and irritable, in no mood for meeting Robert and hearing all about what he and Cathy had said and done last night—because she had a feeling he was sure to tell her, if she encouraged him in the slightest way. Let him go hang.

She'd put on her jeans and the high-top leather boots she'd worn to the airport in Toronto; on the flight down she'd been able to change from them into her new sling-backs, but now that she was going riding, she was glad she still had the boots. Their high heels would let her hold the stirrups better.

It was going to be a hot day. She wished she'd brought a hat. With a final check of herself in a long mirror she left.

There were grooms at the stables when she got there.

"I'd like to go riding. Can I have a horse?"

"Yes, miss. Take any horse."

They were all beautiful. She felt slowly better as she walked past the stalls, looking into every one. The intelligent ears flickered as each horse returned her inspection, sizing her up, wondering if it was the one to be chosen.

"I'd like this one."

"Miss, that's Tiger." The groom's voice was filled with awe. "Tiger is one lively horse, miss. You sure you want this one?"

The horse called Tiger *was* sort of impressive-looking. He held his head high, his ears straight up, and looked Carol Anne over with as much interest as if it was he who was going to decide whether or not she should ride him. Stung by the groom's concern and by Tiger's somewhat supercilious stare, Carol Anne answered sharply.

"That's the horse I want. Bring him into the yard when he's saddled." She left the stable without another word.

Outside in the sunlight she began to have second thoughts. Though she was a good rider, she hadn't been on horseback for months, not since last spring, when she'd rented a horse from a riding stable for a morning. Should she have listened to the groom's advice? Was it too late to change her mind?

Tiger was led out from the stables with a high-stepping gait, his hooves clattering on the cobbles. He looked Carol Anne over once more, then snorted contemptuously, tossing his head while the groom cried "Whoah there!" He led the big black stallion over to a mounting block, nudging the horse's ribs with his stomach to move him into place.

Carol Anne suddenly felt terrified.

But she daren't show fear in front of the grooms. So she raised her chin, mounted the block, put a foot in the stirrup and swung into the saddle with all the outward assurance of someone who'd gone riding on fierce-looking horses every morning of her life. The groom handed her the reins.

Tiger stood there.

She'd half-expected him to rear and buck and try to throw her off the moment she was on his back. But he just stood there, doing his best to make her look and feel foolish.

She shook the reins. He lifted his head, swung it around and looked at her with one large round flickering eyeball. She shook the reins again, and kicked him lightly with her heels. "Come on, Tiger?"

Even as she said it, Carol Anne realized her command sounded more like a question than an order. But it worked anyway. Sedately the big horse moved away from the mounting block, lifting his feet like a trotter, striking sparks from the cobblestones when he brought his feet down. Luckily he was headed in the direction Carol Anne wished to go, so she held the reins loosely, letting him move along at his own pace.

When they got to where the path from the stableyard joined the manor house driveway, Tiger stopped, turned around, lifted his head and neighed derisively at the three grooms who were assembled near the stable door, watching. Carol Anne blushed furiously. She hauled at the reins, pulling the big animal's head around, and kicked him hard in the ribs. He allowed it. He ambled off down the driveway as if he had all day, stopping every so often to nibble at tasty clumps of grass. Each time he did so, Carol Anne jerked his head back up and kicked him in the ribs again. This, she realized, was going to be a contest of wills. She wanted to go for a ride, and Tiger just wanted to go for a stroll and eat anything he came across.

"Well, we'll see about that," Carol Anne told him.

Shreds of mist hung from the bushes in the driveway wherever the rising sun had failed to dissipate them. The sun itself was warm against her face. Already Carol Anne's brow was beaded with perspiration, partly from the sun, partly from the effort of trying to control Tiger.

The driveway sloped gently down, turning to follow the soft contours of the hill, and always there was another bend ahead so that she couldn't see the fields because of the flanking trees and bushes. She wanted to get Tiger out onto the open fields before she really let him know who was boss. Once, when he bent his head again to eat, she thought she caught a glimpse of Find-your-man Hill through the tree branches, but she couldn't be sure. She looked carefully, searching for the little bower on the hilltop, but couldn't really say she'd seen it.

She hauled Tiger's head up again and dragged him away from what he'd found. And this time, all at once, the roadway straightened out after the inevitable bend and the trees fell back, and there, spreading away at her feet for miles, were the far-reaching acres of the estate farms, with the road now cutting through them as straight as an arrow. The asphalt of the driveway became a hard-packed gravel surface where the driveway met the road. Her heart overflowed at the sight of the fields ahead. Now she would ride.

She kicked her heels harder than she'd done before into Tiger's flanks, and leaning over, yelled in his quivering ear.

"Yahoooo!"

It worked. With a snort of fury Tiger leaped ahead; she had to cling hard with her knees to stay in the saddle. Tiger bounded away along the road at a thundering gallop, rapidly eating up the yards, determined to give Carol Anne a run that would hold her for months. Luckily the road was straight. Because even when she pulled on the reins, Tiger took no heed; he was galloping close to the ditch on the right-hand side, and Carol Anne would have felt safer if he was more in the middle of the road. She tugged harder, but his head wouldn't budge. She tried pulling back on the reins to slow him down, but if anything, he just seemed to go faster, and it was as much as she could do just to hang on to her seat. She began to panic.

"Whoa, Tiger," she yelled, but the wind of their passing caught the words from her lips and threw them away. "Whoa!" she yelled as soon as she'd caught her breath again.

Tiger wasn't slowing down; he seemed to be galloping in a frenzy, his gait uneven, his head tossing dangerously. Foam flew from his mouth. Carol Anne had given up trying to control him and was concentrating all her efforts on staying in the saddle. She didn't hear anything but the thunder of Tiger's hoofbeats. She certainly didn't hear the new thunder as Robert's bay mare came up on her near side; her first warning he was near was when his horse's head came into view to her left. She was so startled she nearly lost her seat at last, looking up and starting to fall just as strong arms reached over and around her waist, clutching her tightly. She was dragged off her saddle, kicking free of the stirrups, throwing her arms around Robert the moment she let go of the reins. He was enormously strong. With one arm he lifted her free and swung her up and around in front of him so that she was sitting part on the saddle and part on the horse, held tightly by his arm against his chest, both legs on the side where Tiger was rapidly drawing away from them, snorting and foam flecked.

Carol Anne could hardly breathe. She was acutely conscious of her heart beating rapidly; she was sure Robert could feel it beating through the thin stuff of her blouse where his arm held her tight. There was a surge of strange feeling tearing through her breast, and she was certain any moment that Robert must notice it in her. She had never felt like this before—it was tremendous, exciting, unreal. Partly it was the vestiges of the fear she'd experienced when she finally realized that Tiger had indeed bolted, and she was his captive, not his rider. Partly it was the feel of Robert so close; she could feel his breath against her ear; she was enveloped in the warmth of him. It was difficult to take a deep breath, or to breathe naturally. One moment she was so filled with remembered terror she could hardly stop herself from turning, burying her face against Robert's chest; the next moment she was suffused with a new terror—the fear that Robert might notice how overexcited she was.

He was fighting to hold on to her and to pull his horse back to a walk at the same time. The mare had in turn become frightened when Robert had plucked Carol Anne off Tiger, and it took all Robert's skill to calm her, hold her steady, talk her down into a walk at last. "Steady, steady, old girl. Steady" he called out over and over, almost into Carol Anne's ear.

And finally the mare did slow down. Tiger was far off now, still galloping, hardly more than a cloud of moving dust in the distance.

"I was so frightened." Carol Anne felt she had to say something or burst. But as she said it, she realized she was no longer afraid. Instead she felt more secure and safe than ever in her life. But it ended abruptly. Robert hauled his horse to a stop, gripped her hard with his arm, lifted her easily off the horse and lowered her to the ground. She stood there looking up at him, feeling lost.

93

"You were a fool to take Tiger when the grooms advised against it. You could have been killed. Now, stay right there while I go catch him."

He was gone before he had finished speaking. Off and already galloping, hot in pursuit of her stubborn, unmanageable horse. She felt bereft. Lost and alone. Unbelievably, she found herself already missing the comfort and security of Robert's strong arm around her. She wished for nothing better than to be back inside its circle.

Her knees were shaking so much she had to sit down. There was nowhere except the edge of the ditch. Tiger had leaped it now and was off in a far field, kicking his heels up, probably in exultation, she thought, in celebration of his victory. Robert was catching up on Tiger rapidly. He slowed the mare to a walk before he reached Tiger, then stopped and dismounted, approaching the stallion on foot with the reins of his own horse in one hand.

Tiger leaped and cavorted, kicking and whinnying, making a great to-do. But he was slowing down. He kept pretty much to one small circle, bounding and leaping like a mad thing within an area of a few yards while Robert approached him.

Robert came close and waited. It looked to Carol Anne as if he was talking to the stallion. And after a while Tiger stopped jumping around. He stood there, flanks heaving, head dropping low, the reins trailing on the ground in front of him while Robert got a little closer.

But as soon as Robert was almost close enough to catch the reins, Tiger moved away. He didn't move quickly, but he moved positively, and only just far enough away so that Robert couldn't grab the reins. He did it two or three times. It was so obvious he knew what he was doing that Carol Anne couldn't help but laugh. And that's when she realized she'd hurt herself. As she burst into laughter, there was a sharp stabbing pain in her side, and the moment she felt the pain, she also realized she was aching in a dozen places; her knees both hurt, but the right knee hurt worse than the other. Her thighs were tender to the touch. But the pain in her side was the worst of all. Now it hurt her to take a deep breath. She held her side tight, just under her breast, to make it easier to breathe. She had to stand up at last because it pained less when she did.

Robert had caught Tiger. He was riding the stallion now, leading the mare behind him by its reins. Both horses were walking, obviously worn out with the chase. Tiger looked quite docile now, as if he'd had his fun and was willing to get back to work, if anybody would let him—or trust him. But he lifted his head when he saw Carol Anne standing by the side of the ditch, and blew heavily through his nostrils in her direction.

"Did you hurt yourself?" There was welcome concern in Robert's voice. Carol Anne had been standing there expecting him to come back and finish the tongue-lashing he'd started to give her before he rode off to catch Tiger. Relief flooded through Carol Anne.

"It's my side mostly; it pains when I breathe. And I think I've scraped my knees somehow."

"You're lucky that's all you did." But even as he spoke, Robert was getting down from his mount, a worried expression on his face. Now Carol Anne wasn't sure what he might say next. But she needn't have worried. Robert came up to her, pulling both horses by their reins, looking about for some place to tie them to. He raised his head and looked into the distance.

"Can you walk?" Carol Anne nodded silently, hoping she could; her knees still felt weak. "Good," he said. "See those trees over there? We'll walk over to them so that I can tie the horses to a branch. I'd better have a look at you."

The trees were in a small clump, like a little piece of parkland, scattered apart from each other, no more than a hundred yards away. They set out. Carol Anne offered to lead the mare once they were over the ditch.

"I'll handle them. You walk ahead."

She did so, very conscious that he must be staring at her, her knees shakier than ever as she wondered if her jeans weren't too tight. Tight jeans were the "in" thing, and it took Carol Anne considerable effort and wriggling to get into hers. He must be staring at them now, she realized, trying not to put any more bounce into her hips than was necessary. The odd thing was that instinctively her hips were acting as if they had a mind of their own. She frowned, trying to walk sedately and in a ladylike manner. But it was hard while her knees were trembling; she was afraid her hips were winning the battle.

"Are you sure I can't lead the mare?"

"Just keep walking. We're nearly there."

His tone was peremptory; there was nothing else to do but what he said. She swayed on toward the trees.

By the time she got there, she was near collapse. Her side pained every time she drew a breath; she could feel something warm trickling from her right knee, and she ached everywhere.

The trees were spaced quite far apart, with coarse grass in between them. She almost fell down at the foot of a broad-trunked tree with branches that suddenly sprouted at right angles to the trunk about ten feet up. She leaned her back against it, trying not to breathe too deeply. Robert was on his knees before her in moments; both horses were tied to a nearby low branch.

"Let me see your knee." Without asking permission he was rolling up her right pant leg. She saw a rip in the cloth above the knee, and a bright stain of red through the rip. Deftly he eased the pants past the hurt. Carol Anne felt a strange wave of emotion.

"I think I remember catching it on the saddle when I . . . when you . . ."

"It doesn't matter where it happened; let's have a look at it." He bent his head low, using his handkerchief to wipe away the blood. Her knees, Carol Anne realized, were trembling visibly. The feel of his hand on one, holding it steady, only seemed to make it worse. She drew an unexpected deep breath, gasping as soon as she'd done so. He looked up, worried.

"What's the matter? Does it hurt?"

"Yes. No. Not my knee. It's when I breathe."

"Oh, heaven." He put down the handkerchief and came closer, his face almost touching her shoulder. She felt his hands flat against her ribs, soothing and soft, but deft and firm.

"Now. Breathe in slowly, and tell me when it hurts." His hands moved over her rib cage, squeezing gently, probing for the pain.

"There," she gasped. "That's where it hurts."

One hand moved behind her back. She closed her eyes, unable to be so near to him without feeling the almost overwhelming urge to collapse against his shoulder and sob against his neck.

His other hand stayed on the spot she'd indicated, the edge of his palm just under her breast. She knew he could feel it there, but he made no sign that he did. He was as professional as any doctor. His fingers gently probed her ribs, seeking for anything that might indicate a fracture. He was very thorough and methodical, testing each rib in turn.

"It could be"—his voice was thoughtful and slow— "that you've fractured a rib. But then again, it could be, quite simply, that you're winded. Tell me, is it getting any worse?"

"No, it isn't. It's sort of fading now."

"Hmmm. Maybe it is just that you're winded," he said with a note of relief in his voice. "Just lie there and don't move. Take it easy. Once you get your wind back, you'll be fine, I hope."

She breathed slowly while he made himself comfortable next to her. Her eyes were closed. It was shaded there, but warm. Insects buzzed about their life's work nearby, but didn't come near them. She could hear the horses chomping at their bits. All was so peaceful.

Gradually the pain subsided completely. She was very aware of him close by, and afraid to open her eyes in case he should be looking into them, seeing deep inside her and discovering how she felt. She was scared her breathing might become rapid and shallow, so she exerted great effort to make it slow, even and measured. Her whole body was quivering, but she forced herself to relax.

And then she felt his lips on hers, softly; the merest touch of a kiss, but a kiss nevertheless. Her heartbeat quickened. The most amazingly pleasurable emotion flooded through her. She opened her eyes. Robert was smiling at her.

"You looked as if you were going to sleep," he told her. "Like a little child."

He stood up, towering over her. "I'd better go and get some help," he announced. "You can't very well ride back like that."

"Oh, but I can," she assured him, getting to her own feet. "My side doesn't hurt anymore at all. And my knee won't stop me riding." The thought of Robert going off and leaving her alone was somehow unbearable. Whatever it cost, she wanted to be with him. So she lied a little. "I was just winded, like you said. I feel right as rain now. But will you let me ride your horse? You can have old Tiger."

She was walking toward the tethered horses even as she spoke, giving him no chance to make any real objection. She just couldn't let him go off alone right now. Not after he had kissed her. And he had made such a light thing of that kiss; perhaps to him it *was* nothing at all—a mere gesture—but to her . . . She couldn't even begin to describe what it meant. She honestly didn't know herself.

"Can I ride your horse?" She looked over her shoulder. Robert was standing where she'd left him, frowning at her.

"You're quite sure you're all right?"

"Cross my heart." She did so, smiling.

They rode away in silence. Robert seemed to be deep in thought. Carol Anne was content to say nothing, if that's the way Robert wanted it.

It was a bright, full day now, the sun high in the sky. She

98

hadn't been in any position to pay attention to her surroundings earlier, when she'd been riding Tiger. The brute had demanded every ounce of her concentration. She looked at the stallion as she remembered the wild ride. He was walking sedately now, as if he'd never so much as dreamt of taking the bit between his teeth and run off like a mad thing. Perhaps he knew perfectly well that Robert wouldn't stand for any such nonsense. Carol Anne smiled to herself.

"They're cutting cane over there. Stop a minute, I want to watch." Robert gestured toward a field where dozens of workers were hacking away at what looked like a burnt-over field, piling the stalks in bunches.

"I'll have to go over to the sugar mill later," Robert said, as if thinking aloud. "Sugar's our big cash crop, and I like to check every step of the harvesting."

"Oh, I'd love to see a sugar mill," Carol Anne said, remembering that the Captain had suggested she might get Robert to show her through it. "Could I come with you?"

He laughed. "Where you have to go is into bed."

"Not on your life! I'm as healthy as old Tiger there. Come on, let's go to the mill."

Truthfully Carol Anne couldn't care in the least about seeing a sugar mill. She just wanted to stay with Robert. So if he wanted to go through a mill or to climb a mountain, that's what she wanted to do too.

He looked her over, frowning. Carol Anne's heart slowed down. Was he going to say no?

"You're no advertisement from *Vogue,* you know. Are you sure you want to be seen looking like that?"

Horrified, she looked down at herself. Her blouse was dirty. Her jeans were ripped; the right leg was still rolled up as far as the knee, protecting the scab that was forming over her cut. Both her arms—bare from above the elbow—were streaked with dust. Her face! Why hadn't she brought a mirror? She must look like a ragamuffin. She raised her eyes to his. He burst out laughing at once.

99

"Carol Anne, the way you look right now, I couldn't take you to a dog fight. Come. We'll get you back to the hotel." He swung Tiger's head around and set off. Reluctantly she had to follow him. They rode in silence, side by side, until abruptly he turned to her.

"Carol Anne? Where did you disappear to last night at the party? I looked all over for you."

She was surprised enough to answer immediately.

"I went to my room. I never thought you'd miss me."

"Why? Did the party bore you?"

"Heavens no. I was having a wonderful time."

"I could see that. You danced with every man there. . . ."

"And with you too, before you began spending all your time with . . ." She stopped in mid-sentence, wishing she could bite her tongue off.

"With Cathy?" Robert ended her thought for her. He was silent for a while. "Yes. I did spend a lot of time with Cathy. I hadn't seen her in ages, don't forget. We had a lot to talk over." Then he laughed aloud, but evidently not at something that he thought was funny. Carol Anne glanced at his face in surprise.

"But you did have a good time at the party," he said.

"I had a marvelous time," Carol Anne lied. "Everything was just perfect."

"Hrrmph," said Robert, as if he didn't believe her completely. She wondered if he could read her mind.

"After Rome and Paris, all this must seem quite tame to you." Robert waved his arm at the fields. "A little get-together on a farm couldn't compare with a dance at some grand hotel on the Riviera."

"Everything is fun in its own way," she answered carefully.

"Cathy was telling me about Rome and Paris. It's a wonder you two haven't bumped into each other before. She says you meet the same people everywhere you go, and"—he adopted a stagy British accent—"it's all so frightfully boring."

100

Carol Anne didn't enlighten him. Her conscience was nudging her, trying to make her tell Robert that she wasn't a globetrotter, that in fact this was her first trip out of Canada because she'd only just started as a travel agent. But she told her conscience to be quiet; there was no way she would have him think she was any less than Cathy McKinnon.

"In some ways I imagine it is boring," Robert mused. "Cathy's life revolves around rather silly competitions now; she got a second place in a slalom event in St. Moritz recently, and she was as proud of it as if she'd won an Olympic medal. She even remembered the mixed-doubles cup we won together, years ago. Insisted we go up to the manor house and find it, because she wants it for her trophy case."

So that's where you two went to last night. Or are you just making excuses? She glanced at his face again, but he didn't look guilty.

"She must have told me a dozen times how it was her play that won," Robert added morosely. "She's changed."

"She's certainly very beautiful."

He turned in his saddle to look at her.

"Every man is attracted to pretty girls," he argued. "Nature makes girls beautiful for just that reason, so that men will want to come close to them. But after the men are attracted—when the girls have got them nearby—then they have to exert some sort of effort to keep them around. Looks alone aren't enough; a girl has to have something more than that."

"Like what, for instance?"

"Oh, the all-inclusive description would be charm, I suppose. Many older women have charm. They may be well past the time when they had good looks, but they still have charm. So quite often you'll see men of all ages talking to charming older women, while pretty girls at the same gathering are left to talk to each other for amusement."

101

"That's interesting. So what's your definition of charm?" It was delightful to hear Robert talk like this; he sounded so serious, even professorial, but in doing so he was letting her peek inside him and find out what made him tick.

"Charm?" He rode in silence for a while, obviously trying to pin down in words the things that went to make up charm in his estimation. He spoke at last. "I think it's the feeling I have when I'm talking to someone, and I realize that they're really interested in me—in what I say and do. Maybe charm is a personal thing between two people. One person can be considered charming by some people, but not by others."

Carol Anne pondered this, and didn't answer. They were near enough to the hill on which the manor house was built to be able to pick out features. The horses had quickened their pace, sensing water and feed close by.

More to the point, she was also wondering if Robert had been trying to tell her something personal when he spoke his opinion about charm in women. She was still tingling from his light kiss. Twice, now, he had kissed her. Did he make a habit of kissing every girl he met? Did it mean anything to him, or was it as casual a thing for him as stopping at each flower was to a bee?

But she dreaded to think things through and find out that Robert really was only a light romantic—or that perhaps this business of kissing people was a local custom, and meant nothing. How much better to cling to the possibility that Robert kissed only her, and only because he wanted to. She tingled again, hugging the thought, and glanced at him as they rode.

He sat so straight and tall in the saddle, moving easily to the motion of the horse, in complete command without even thinking about riding, because he had ridden for so much of his life. He and the horse were one. Every inch of him demonstrated assurance and confidence, as if he always knew what he was doing and meant everything he said.

So, then, did he mean her to understand something special when he spoke about charm? She was confused, thinking about it. And, she realized with the slightest of involuntary grimaces, she still hurt all over from that wild ride on Tiger.

"Are you sure you're feeling all right?" He must have caught sight of her face when the ache went through her. There was concern in his question, and it somehow made the aches vanish, like a wonder drug. So it was with genuine truth that she assured him she was fine.

Up ahead she could see the roof of the manor house poking above the trees. Off to one side of it was the peak of the hill with Find-your-man's pretty bower just under it; she could make out the head of the statue that stood there. And a little below that was a red-roofed white cottage that she'd never noticed before. Before it was a low-walled patio overlooking the farmlands they had just ridden from. And even though she had never seen it before, she had the strangest feeling that, actually, she had, sometime long ago. She turned to Robert.

"Is that where you live, up in that cottage?"

"That's it. My home away from home."

She reined to a stop to get a better look. "What a terrific view you must have."

Robert smiled at her over his shoulder as he rode ahead. "Come on up and have a look around if you want."

I'd love to." But before she urged her horse on, she looked long and hard at the cottage above her, and at the acres of gentle, wooded hillside in which it was set, while an idea began to germinate in her mind.

A flagstoned path led away from the driveway toward Robert's cottage. She must have missed seeing it this morning because it was so tucked away between the trees. They both dismounted there, draping the reins over the horses' necks.

"They'll find their own way home," Robert announced,

slapping big Tiger on the rump. "All they want is their oats and a bucket of water. Giddyap, there. Off you go."

The horses ambled away, picking up their pace as they went up the drive, scenting their stables. She and Robert stood there to watch and make certain they didn't stray until the animals had rounded the first bend, then turned to follow the flagstone path.

It was heavily scented in there between the bushes. Carol Anne sniffed happily, nose in the air, and was about to ask Robert what was causing the scent when he answered her unspoken question.

"Frangipani," he said. "Most of the hillside is covered with it. My mother had it planted because she liked the smell. It is nice, though, don't you think?"

Once again Carol Anne had that strange feeling of *déjà vu*. It was as if she'd been along this path before, as if she'd been bathed in this lovely scent before. She wondered if she had second sight. But perhaps, somewhere else, she had smelled it, and that was what was tickling the depths of her memory. Even so, she "knew" what the first sight of the cottage would be when they rounded the last bend. And it was exactly as she had "remembered" it. She was brought to a stop by what she saw, and an involuntary gasp escaped her. Robert turned in concern, looking at her worriedly. "Are you all right?"

"I'm fine, really. I just want to stop here a minute and look." But Robert came back, and stood beside her, evidently not convinced that she was as well as she claimed. In the easiest, most assuring of manners he slipped his arm around her waist and held her to his side. It made her blood race, but she didn't try to move away. Perhaps he really only meant to support her if she felt weak, she realized. But perhaps . . . perhaps he just wanted to hold her like that.

But she really did want to look at his cottage. It backed against the hillside, with red flagstones making a wide patio in front of it, ending at the low stone wall. Part of the cottage roof overhung the patio so that the living room

104

was an indoor-outdoor affair, with sliding glass doors that could be closed off in bad weather. Today the doors were wide open. Comfortable wicker furniture was scattered about, indoors and out.

"I think we'd better get you where we can take another look at you," Robert said in a low voice. His arm around her tightened slightly, holding her close while they walked on. Her shoulder, she realized, fitted exactly under his arm. As if it belonged there. She let him lead her onto the patio.

But when they got there, he made no move to take his arm away. And she made no move to break free.

They were facing the valley spread out for them below, but neither saw it. Carol Anne could feel nothing but the sensation of being held close against Robert; everything else was a bright blur, and nothing else mattered.

"Would you like to lie down and rest? There's a couch I can drag out here, if you want."

She didn't answer. All she wanted was to stand there, just the way they were. And how could she tell Robert that?

He must have sensed it, because all at once his other arm was around her too, and she was being held close, his face in her hair. And now one hand came under her chin to lift it, and his lips were on hers at last, but not lightly, as they had been by the swimming pool and under the tree in the lands below. Now they were hungry and urgent, and she discovered that she had slipped her arms around his neck and was kissing him back just as urgently, while the world spun dizzily, faster than it was meant to, making her so weak that she would have fallen if his strong arms hadn't been around her.

There was a discreet cough somewhere nearby. Carol Anne didn't hear it, but Robert must have, because she felt him break away, surprising her. But one arm stayed around her as he turned.

A black man stood in the doorway with a tray on which were two tinkling glasses. And when they looked at him his face broke into a smile as big as the sun. Carol Anne gathered her wits together and smiled back. But Robert, thank heaven, kept that one arm around her, otherwise she might have collapsed.

"Welcome home Mr. Robert. Welcome, Miss Todd." The man came toward them, proffering the tray.

"Hello, Harold," Robert answered, then smiled down on Carol Anne. "Harold's Charlene's husband, you know."

She slipped easily into the polite and impersonal atmosphere which had suddenly replaced the confusing, unbelievable one of moments before. In a way, she was glad it had gone. What would have happened if it hadn't?

She smiled again at Harold, at the same time stepping free of Robert's encircling arm.

"Oh? Charlene's very proud of you, Harold. She tells me all about you."

Harold laughed in a deep rumble, making the glasses tinkle. Robert took one and handed it to Carol Anne, then took his own.

"Cheers," he said. "How d'you like my little place?"

Thirstily she drained her glass. "Let me have a fast look around," she said as she handed it back to Harold, "then I'll leave you to your bath and go jump into my own. If I don't, the Captain won't let me set foot in the manor house again."

Robert slumped into a creaking chair and waved an arm in permission. "Help yourself," he said. "Take your time. I'm just going to sit here and stick my feet out." But he squeaked the chair around on the stones until it was facing the cottage, showing every sign of planning to enjoy watching Carol Anne investigate his home. "Go ahead, I'll just sit here."

The cottage was spacious, roomy and modern. And yet it was also compact, not taking up very much room on the hillside. It had the huge living room she'd noticed first, and a fair-sized bedroom. The bathroom was up-to-date, and there was a bar in the living room, with a refrigerator.

The only thing it didn't have was a kitchen. Carol Anne inspected it thoroughly, her mind filled with the same idea she'd had when she'd first glimpsed the cottage, while they were riding home. Her face was thoughtful when she came back out onto the patio.

"You look as if you've found dirty socks under my bed."

"What?" Then she smiled, realizing how she must look. "No, of course not. It's just that I'm thinking something out."

Robert was just finishing his drink. He stood up.

"There's another pathway behind the cottage; leads you up to the manor house. Let me show you the way."

The new path led more steeply upward, culminating in a flight of stone steps that brought her onto the courtyard. They walked together to the top of the steps.

"See you at dinner?" He smiled. "I'd better get back to work." She watched him turn and walk away, and suddenly she realized how tired and completely exhausted she was. She felt grubby and weary. Her knees were sore from gripping the horse. Her hands were sore; she was sore all over. But she was happy, definitely happy; tonight at dinner there was no chance at all of Cathy McKinnon being there.

Charlene had her bath ready. Carol Anne could have kissed her for it, but instead she peeled off her clothes, dropped them outside the door, and slid luxuriously into the steaming water, releasing a huge sigh as she gratefully closed her eyes. How utterly, deliciously weary can a body be? she wondered.

She was aware that she had some serious thinking to do. Was there a better time or place for it? She lay there, soaking out the aches, going over the situation, working out the answers. There are some things a girl has to do that she may not like, she told herself, but she has to do them anyway. Like it or not, they still have to be done.

For a start, I've only been here two days. So even if it feels as if I've been here forever, the fact is that I haven't.

And even worse, in another day or two I'll have to leave again and go home. Home? Visions of swirling snow; people clutching their coat collars to their necks as they hurried for subways and streetcars. She slowly shook her head. That couldn't be home.

But it is. That's where you live and that's where you're going back to, very soon. So face it.

She did, most reluctantly, shutting her mind to the present.

Well, she asked herself at last, so I'm going home soon. Then what?

Then you have to make a report to Mr. Roxlet about the Captain's hotel, and after that you take life up where you left it off; this interlude has just been a holiday, that's all, and after you've been home awhile, it will fade away into just a very pleasant memory.

But does it have to?

Yes! It has to. What right have you to come here for a couple of days and disrupt people's lives? To put it bluntly, what right do you think you have to try to step in between Robert Innes and Cathy McKinnon?

At last she was facing it, the one problem that she hadn't been able to put into words until now.

She felt close to tears. It had been a marvelous morning; so many times she could have wished that a moment could go on forever. Why couldn't this day be just one of hundreds more just like it? I love Robert Innes, she insisted, so why must I go?

Love, said her conscience scornfully. You've only known him two days. And you think it's love? What does it matter anyway; he loves Cathy McKinnon, and obviously she's set her mind on getting him. She'll be here next week, and all the weeks afterward. But you'll be a thousand miles away in another country. So forget about love. Face reality.

But Cathy's not right for Robert! She's a spendthrift and a—what was it Dino called her?—a gadabout. Robert

108

needs every penny for his farms just now, so Cathy would be just a huge liability with her trips and clothes and . . .

A thought struck her. She frowned.

Cathy did appear to spend a lot of money. That dress she'd worn to the party must have cost hundreds. Even the shoes she wore were expensive. And if you considered what it costs to fly around Europe to the most popular places. Hadn't Robert mentioned St. Moritz? And Dino mentioned Estoril in Portugal?

Where did she get the money?

Her father, Doug McKinnon, was a penny pincher. Surely she didn't get it from him? And in any case, according to the Captain, Doug McKinnon was having as hard a time as all the other farmers in the valley, trying to make ends meet, so he couldn't be supporting his daughter because he just didn't have the money.

But somehow Doug McKinnon had found the money to buy seventy acres of land from the Innes estate. And, if her memory served her properly, he'd also bought land from other farmers recently.

So he must have extra money. Even if, as the Captain had said, McKinnon borrowed money from banks to buy the land, he still had to be able to repay it. Which meant he must be making more from his farms than anyone else was, because that's where his income had to come from. So how did he do it? Did he have so much more land than anyone else that he made more?

She sat up in the bathtub so suddenly that she slopped water over the side. Slowly she began soaping herself, puzzling over the problem of McKinnon's money.

I'd like to see his account books, she thought, the years of bookkeeping experience coming to the fore.

But that was impossible. And, more to the point, it was none of her business. Absolutely none of her business whatsoever.

Your business, she told herself severely, is the hotel. Your good new friend the Captain wants it to be a success.

Mr. Roxlet would be pleased if it was a success. You yourself would like it to be a success, and if it isn't a success, Robert's farms will have to be sold. So concentrate on the hotel. What can you do to make sure it's a success? Think, girl, think!

By the time she had finished toweling herself thoroughly dry, Carol Anne knew what she had to do.

Carol Anne had lunch alone on the veranda. The Captain was probably still at the sugar mill, and Robert had gone back to work and wouldn't be home till dinnertime. She ate lightly, even though she was ravenous after her energetic and exciting morning. Her side had stopped paining completely; probably she had been merely winded, as Robert had thought. Her right knee ached a little, but that was all. Her other aches and pains had been soothed away in her bathtub.

There was so much work to be done. She daren't eat as much as she felt like, because inevitably she'd be tired if she did, and would almost have to take a nap. And this afternoon she needed to be clear-minded and wide-awake.

After lunch she strolled through the hotel's grounds, making sure she'd noted everything on the questionnaire that was important. But her steps took her without planning to up to the crest of Find-your-man Hill, because her mind was already up there, calculating and planning.

She'd brought a pen and some extra paper. She sat on the stone bench where the Captain had proposed to his lady and made calculations on the paper, standing up once in a while to peer over the shrubs and look down the hillside. From where she stood she could see the roof of Robert's cottage below. It gave her an odd feeling of possessiveness, but she squashed it as fast as it arose; she had work to do, the work she'd been sent here for.

Her eyes measured the rest of the hill. There were many acres of it, all gently undulating land, sloping very gradually downward. It was tree-covered, but not a thick forest by any means. Robert's cottage didn't seem to have

110

displaced any of the trees when it was built. Rather, it nestled in among them. And though it was a relatively spacious home, it really didn't take up very much room where it stood. Her eyes roamed over the rest of the hillside; then she sat down on the warm stone bench and began to set down columns of figures.

She was so still and quiet, working there, that the many creatures who were used to spending their lives around that bower lost the fear they'd caught when she first appeared among them, and resumed the tiny burdens of their little lives. Carol Anne realized, as she figured, that there was a very good reason for calling hummingbirds that name. She looked up to watch one, its body quite motionless while its wings blurred into nothing, as it deftly poked its long beak into a purple flower, seeking nectar. The sound of the wings was a distinct hum, like a note from a musical instrument. She smiled in happiness for it. And as she smiled, the miniature bird flew off faster than her eyes could follow it. Carol Anne returned to her figures.

This was the kind of work she found easy, because she'd been trained for it and she liked it, having always had a good head for mathematics. It pleased her to cost things out and discover the point at which they became profitable, or, alternately, so likely to be unprofitable that they shouldn't be attempted. From the experience of her two years in the accounting division of the agency Carol Anne dredged up costs: the last brochure she'd worked on, for the Inverurie Hotel in Bermuda, was roughly the sort of brochure this new venture would need, and she knew exactly what it cost to produce and distribute. From the notes she'd made on Mr. Roxlet's questionnaire, she worked out just what should be advertised on the brochure, and even jotted down some notes as to headlines and copy.

But the mass of the figures she was writing down concerned a new idea, one that had come to her as she stood on the patio of Robert's cottage that morning, and which she was now refining and costing out to make certain it would work.

If her idea worked, the hotel would be a roaring success. And if it was a success, Robert's farms were saved. She worked steadily on, and late in the afternoon she smiled, putting down her pen. It would work. The farms were safe.

Then a little voice within her asked, "Safe? Yes, but for whom? For Cathy?" The smile left Carol Anne's face.

She allowed herself to relax. She lifted her eyes from the page and stared off into the distance. She couldn't see Robert, or even the Captain; they both must be still in the sugar mill, which she could see, sharp and plain in the distance.

Robert, she thought. Oh, what a big problem you are. Here's your father breaking his heart to try to save your precious farms by turning his own home into a hotel, and you fight him tooth and nail every step of the way. Here's me trying to help your father make his hotel a success, and you practically hate me for it. And both of us are slaving away at this venture strictly for you. Just you. If it wasn't for you, your father would probably give in and let things slide. If it wasn't for your father, I wouldn't even be here trying to help.

And what will you do when, despite your objections, we win, and make this venture a success? Why, you'll probably marry Cathy McKinnon if she has anything to say about it, and in a year or two—five at the most—she'll have spent every penny you have and you'll be as badly off as if we hadn't even tried to help you at all.

Robert Innes, you are a big fool!

Tears welled up into her eyes. The sugar mill became blurry in the distance. She didn't blink the tears away. Her anger wouldn't allow her to acknowledge they were even there.

I love you, you big fool. But there's nothing I can do about it. Yes, I'll admit it, I love you. I've loved you since that first night, when you were in the ditch with that

112

donkey, and I could see your big, calm hands soothing the poor thing, and I knew it after you lifted me off Tiger's back. But you don't love me. You don't think any more of me than you did of that donkey; this morning, when you put those big hands against my breast, I could just as well have been another animal in pain that you were tending to.

But you did kiss me.

Despite her growing anger, Carol Anne suddenly laughed, spilling the tears down her cheeks. At least I'm more to him than a donkey, she thought; he didn't kiss the donkey. And again she laughed, her spirits rising rapidly. All the birds and insects which had crept back into the little bower flew away, unsure of how to take her new attitude.

But it was true, she *did* love him, and it *was* an impossible situation, because neither had he shown in any way that he was even aware of her feeling for him, nor was there any hint that he in turn felt anything for her. And in any case there was so little time. And to cap it all there was Cathy McNasty, Carol Anne remembered grimly. The magnificently beautiful Cathy McKinnon, who had known Robert for years and could afford to wait until she got him. And who would lead him a dog's life when she did get him. It was all so unfair. So wrong. But there was nothing she could do about it.

All she could do was what she was sent down here to do. Well, so be it, she thought. At least nobody will be able to fault me for that, because I know how to make this hotel venture work and pay for itself.

She sat there alone until the sun was a huge red disk touching the ground on the horizon and the hordes of daytime birds and insects began to creep away to make way for their brethren, the tiny, chirruping night creatures.

Chapter Seven

Carol Anne hesitated at the entrance to the bar. Her heart gave a small leap. Only Robert was there, handsome in jacket and slacks, wearing a shirt opened at the neck. There was no sign of the Captain. Robert rose to his feet, smiling politely.

"Father's still going over his accounts," he told her as she came forward. "He'll join us later."

He held her chair for her, and no sooner was she sitting than the barman brought her a familiar-looking tall glass, half-filled with fruit.

"Your fruit punch," Robert smiled. "I ordered it before you arrived."

"Thank you. I'll miss these when I'm back in Toronto."

His face clouded momentarily. "That won't be for a while, will it?" She glanced at him in surprise. Was he going to miss her? Or was something else on his mind? She took a sip of her drink.

"Sooner or later I'll have to go," she told him, feeling sad again. But she shooed the thought away; she'd gone over all that in her bath. "As soon as I've learned all I can about the hotel, anyway."

"That's what I wanted to tell you; I've decided to help you and Father with your hotel plans."

She raised her eyebrows, unbelieving. He laughed. "It's

true, so don't look so surprised; as long as there was a chance of stopping the venture, I tried to. It was natural, wasn't it? I didn't think it would work, and all I could see was a terrible waste of money. But after talking to people last night, and seeing your reaction when that Dino person was shown to be the designer of the hotel, well, it seems as if it's too far along to be stopped easily. It would be like throwing a log into the machinery now, and wouldn't help me or anybody."

She looked questioningly into his face. If only she could believe him. It had been so awful to know that father and son were quarreling over this venture.

He was talking again, his voice low and earnest.

"Anyway, I've decided to help in any way I can short of letting the farms suffer."

"Robert. Who designed your cottage?"

"The one I live in? Why, I did, as a matter of fact. It's no architectural-award winner, of course; quite a simple building. Why? What did you have in mind?"

"If what I'm thinking about is practical, perhaps you could leave the manor-house rooms strictly for the use of the family," she said.

"Twenty huge rooms for just two men? That's silly. That's why I moved out in the first place and built my cottage. Nothing but waste, the way it was; armies of servants plus all the overhead and upkeep, just to look after two men."

She looked down at her drink when she spoke next, not wishing to look into his face.

"I imagine you'll be getting married someday. Your wife will want the use of some of those rooms."

"Marriage? That could be years away. I've got to put the farms on a paying basis before I can even think of anything like that."

Carol Anne felt the strangest mixture of happiness and disappointment. If he was in no rush to get married, that meant, at least, that he hadn't been thinking of Cathy McKinnon in that light. But then . . . She forced her mind back to business. But Robert was speaking again before she could get a word out.

"Then, on the other hand," he was saying, "it's true. I don't suppose any man really gets away with *planning* to be married at a certain date or time. I imagine he's at the mercy of the young lady who decides to lay him by the heels."

"Do you really believe that?"

"Well, they say it takes two to tango, but they both have to want to; and one of them has to suggest it in the first place"—he laughed that attractive laugh again—"and these days, as often as not, it's the lady who makes the suggestion, so I read in the books they're writing."

Carol Anne laughed too. It was so pleasant to be with him when he was in a good mood. "I don't believe it's only *these* days," she argued, "I think it's always been that way."

"Then I'll have to watch my step, I suppose. Can't afford to be trapped just yet."

"Not until the farms are paying for themselves," she added, confident that this was what he was about to say. But he looked surprised. Even so, he didn't look displeased; there had been a catch in her throat when she saw his eyebrows raise. She wanted desperately to keep him in this pleasant mood.

"I didn't know you cared about my farms," he mused.

"Of course I do. I mean, well, *you* care about them, and I don't want anything to happen that would . . . well . . ." She began to blush in her confusion. He smiled at her, looking into her eyes.

"You look very lovely when you blush,"

"Oh, shush! I just tripped over my own tongue, that's all."

"Then you must trip over it more often. It becomes you." His voice was mocking, but not cruel. She shook her head, letting her hair fall more smoothly down her back.

"I think we should talk about the hotel," she told him

116

seriously. "It's very important that we plan things properly."

"I make my own plans very carefully indeed."

His eyes were twinkling. Carol Anne had the feeling he was teasing her. Once again she had to force her mind back to the work at hand. She put on a straight face and looked businesslike.

"We know this place will need more guest rooms," she said matter-of-factly. "The bar and dining-room facilities are excellent. The tennis courts and the golf course and riding stables—all these things are very good and necessary. But they'll be wasted if you don't have enough rooms in your hotel to fill with guests so that the other things can be used."

"So what are you suggesting?"

She didn't answer right away, putting her thoughts in order. "Robert? Would it be hard to build other cottages on the hillside where you've got yours?"

"Not really; just a matter of money. All the plumbing lines are already there, because I had to put them in for my own place. That was the hardest part of the job. But now they're all in, I could easily build another couple of cottages. That was the idea, in the first place, to build another cottage for the Captain, so that we could close up the manor house for good."

"How many more cottages could you build?"

"As many as you want. It's just a matter of money." His face showed that he'd suddenly realized what she was driving at. "Oh," he said. "Now I see." He looked very thoughtful.

"Can't be done," he said at last. "Two, or perhaps three more cottages is all I could find the money for. How many were you thinking of?"

"Forty. There's plenty of room on the hillside for them."

He whistled softly, shaking his head. "I do admire your spirit. But forty cottages? It would cost thousands. We just don't have that kind of money."

117

Carol Anne had thought it all out. It was just a matter of finding the most diplomatic way to say what had to be said. Once again she marshaled her thoughts.

"Tell me," she began, "are all the upstairs rooms as filled with furniture as mine is?"

"We moved a lot of things up to the rooms from down here when the architect remodeled. I suppose they are, yes."

"The same sort of furniture as there is in my room? I mean, old and . . . well, quite attractive, but old?"

"Everything's been in the family for years." He laughed again, that deep soft laugh that always thrilled her. "Generations of Inneses bought furniture as the house grew, and nobody ever had the heart to throw any of it out."

"You must have a sentimental spot in your heart for it."

"Oh, not really; it's just the furniture."

"But there must be a lot of pieces that you really care for."

"I imagine so, but I've never thought about it; it was always there, that's all."

"Would you miss any of it if it weren't there?"

"Damned if I know. What are you driving at?"

"A lot of those pieces of furniture would qualify as antiques, I'd guess. Anything a hundred years old or older would. And anything that's beautifully hand-crafted."

"Lots of both sorts around. I'd imagine nearly all of it was either one or the other. I don't think Father ever bought any furniture, and I know I haven't, so it's all at least fifty years old. And I know for a fact there are still a few pieces belonging to the family founder around, Don Carlos José María Iñez." The Spanish words rolled easily off his tongue. "Then there are things brought over from England by various women who married into the family. They're all around somewhere."

"There's an awful lot of money being paid for antiques these days," she ventured. Now was the time to find out if

118

he'd go for her idea. Her heart was racing, waiting for his response.

"What? You mean, sell the furniture? It's undignified!" The cold note was back in his voice. She hastened to explain her idea.

"I'm not suggesting you sell any *furniture*," she argued. "What I'm thinking about is organizing the world's greatest *antique* sale of the year, right here in the manor house. Naturally, the manor house would contribute quite a number of antiques. But I'm depending on there being quite a lot of pieces available from the other old homes in the valley, too. It would be quite a job, rounding up the best pieces from the other homes, making sure you got them at the right price. And what I'm thinking is that you could open the hotel officially by having the antique sale.

"I know an auction gallery in Toronto that would leap at the idea. They'd send their best man down here the minute they heard about it, to assess what's available and even give you an estimate on what you could hope to get from the sale. And if they thought it would work, I know that Mr. Roxlet could work with them to organize it all. Think of it; people from all over the world would come, and they'd all be paying their own way while they're here. You'd have a hotel opening that would get worldwide attention. And you'd raise enough money so that you could afford to pay for the cottages you'd build to house the antique dealers in."

"But . . . Are you trying to tell me people would pay that much for our old sticks of furniture?"

She leaned over the table. "My own apartment in Toronto is furnished with things I picked up at auction galleries. I know what people are paying for old things. Thousands of dollars, quite often, for furniture that's old or handmade. It's because that sort of furniture just isn't made anymore. Believe me, I've seen it done."

"It all sounds unbelievable." He shook his head. "And

most undignified," he added. "I don't think I care for the idea." But the bad tone wasn't in his voice; he just sounded as if he needed convincing. Carol hastened to do that.

"How much do you need to build a cottage?" she asked quickly. "Just one cottage."

"Oh, about a thousand dollars, now that the plumbing lines are in. That's not counting labor, of course."

"Two pieces of furniture will buy you one cottage," she told him solemnly, nodding her head. "And one cottage will return you about"—she did some rapid mental calculations—"ten or so thousand dollars a year. That's gross. You'd have expenses, of course, out of that." She added the last part as a warning, because the moment she'd mentioned "ten thousand dollars a year" as the income from a cottage, Robert's eyes had lit up.

"Hello, m'dear . . . Robert. Sorry to keep you waiting." The Captain came into the room, calling out his hearty greeting. "I won't have anything," he said to the waiter as he passed. "Might have a drop of wine at dinner instead."

The gong sounded as a punctuation to his words.

"See, we're just in time for it," he added, proffering Carol Anne his arm as she rose from her seat. "You two look like you've been having a cozy chat. What have you been talking about?"

"Cottages," said Carol Anne as she took his arm.

"How's that?" The Captain stopped.

"I was just working out for Robert what the income from a cottage might be, per year," she explained.

"And she wants to build forty of them, Father."

"Forty? Where'd we get the money?"

"Carol Anne has got it all worked out," answered Robert diplomatically. "Perhaps she'll explain it all at dinner."

"True. You'll have to do that. Ten thousand a year, you say? Jamaican or American dollars?" The Captain pulled back a chair for Carol Anne. The waiter was already holding another for him when he was ready.

"I'd worked it out in Canadian dollars, but they're roughly on a par with American." She sat down, taking the menu the waiter offered her.

"Hmmmm," mused the Captain. "I think that calls for a spot of wine. I'll make it champagne if you can tell me how we can pay for those forty cottages Robert mentioned. She did say forty?" He turned to his son, who nodded, smiling back. "Hmmmmm." He scanned the wine list.

"Father . . .," Robert chuckled. "I think you might as well make it champagne. Go ahead, Carol Anne, tell him."

She told the Captain, delighted to know that Robert was on her side, ready to counter any of his objections. His eyes widened and his mouth dropped open at one point; he closed it with an audible click when he realized what he must look like.

"My dear girl," he said in awe, "you have the most marvelous head on your shoulders. Just like m'dear wife used to be. Where do you get all these brilliant ideas? Why don't I think of them? And what's more to the point, why didn't that architect fellow think of cottages?"

"Possibly because he never saw Robert's. I didn't think of them myself until I saw it, and all the hillside not really being used for anything; I could just *see* forty cottages up there, and because of all the trees, they'd be quite hidden from view. Yet they would all have a magnificent view over the valley—like forty separate Find-your-man Hills." She was so enthusiastic the words just tumbled out of her. Robert had caught her spirit too.

"Carol Anne thinks we could dispense with renting out the rooms upstairs, if we had cottages." His voice held a mixture of satisfaction and relief, as if all along renting out those rooms had been something he couldn't bring himself to accept.

"But what happens to the manor house, m'dear? Do we just leave it empty?" The Captain sounded disappointed.

"Goodness no. All the ground floor will be used by the guests. Their cottages won't have kitchens, so they'll have to come here for their meals; you'll need the veranda lunch tables as well as the indoor dining room with forty cottages. Don't forget, you'll have families—six or seven people sometimes—in some of the cottages. You could very easily be thinking of two hundred or more guests during peak times. Many of them will want to have breakfast on their patios, but they'll have to come here for dinner at least. Maybe you could serve lunch picnic-style, out by the pool.

"And the bar will be used, of course. Also all the other downstairs rooms. It's only the upstairs rooms that you'd keep private, just for the family's use."

"All those empty rooms upstairs?" The Captain's eyebrows rose. Robert laughed. "Carol Anne thinks I'll need them all when I get married."

"Damned good idea. Marriage. Do you the world of good. Keep you from working yourself to death. Hmmmm. Be nice to see those rooms filled with family. Been a long time." He leaned across the table and patted Carol Anne's hand, winking at her. "Don't you think it's time Robert got married, m'dear?" His white mustache points curled upward. Carol Anne felt herself blushing again. "Just what the blighter needs. Get himself a clever young woman. Solve a lot of problems, truly it would."

"Now, Father, can't you see you're embarrassing Carol Anne? Here, let me fill the glasses. Let's have a toast to Carol Anne's cottages." Robert tipped the last of the champagne into the glasses. He and his father raised them high while Carol Anne smiled.

"To the cottages."

"And to Carol Anne," Robert added as his eyes met hers."

"Amen."

122

They both downed the champagne. Robert looked around as if about to throw his glass into a fireplace.

"Don't you dare!" Carol Anne was shocked."

"I think I ought to. You've accomplished wonders since you've been here. Why, just up until a day or so ago the Captain and I were practically at each other's throats. You've ended that, for one thing. And as for convincing me that the hotel idea would work, why, I'd never have believed it."

"Too true, m'dear. Absolute marvel is what you are."

"Now you're going to make me lightheaded, both of you, so stop it." She made her tone light, but tears were smarting behind her sparkling eyes; these two were such wonderful men, and they were so nice to her. If either of them spoke another word, she'd just break down.

But the fates were smiling on her. They'd eaten a delicious dinner of rare roast beef while they'd been talking, and now the waiter came to clear away their plates, effectively putting a halt to further conversation for the moment.

"Would the lady or the gentlemen care for any dessert, sir?"

"Dessert? Good idea. What have you got?"

"A trifle, sir."

Carol Anne was about to ask what sort of trifle his dessert might be, never having heard of the dish before. But the Captain spoke for all of them. "I think that's a splendid idea. Trifle it is. All right with you, m'dear?"

"It sounds very interesting."

She waited in anticipation, because she was still hungry, having enjoyed the roast beef so much; she wished she'd asked for more. But the dessert would help still the craving.

The waiter was back almost immediately with tall glasses. He set one in front of her on her plate. Inside was an intriguing mixture. On the very top was a cherry, set on a spike of whipped cream. Beneath that was fresh fruit, separated from a layer of canned apricots by a slice of yellow sponge cake, and under the apricots was another slice of cake—fruitcake, heavy and solid. An aromatic, delicious sauce had been poured over everything. It smelled divine, and slightly alcoholic. Carol Anne gazed at the trifle in awe. Robert chuckled at her expression.

"There must be a billion calories in that," she said in a reverent voice.

"Eat it anyway," he urged her. "Tell yourself it's good for you." He was already spooning into his own dessert, enjoying every bit of it. "Besides, I don't imagine you're the kind of woman that puts on weight."

"That's true," she said, bravely picking up her spoon, "or at least I hope it is, because I'm going to eat it all."

It was the happiest meal she'd had so far in the manor house. And she knew that both men were as content with the evening as she was. Each was glad their feud had ended; each acted toward her as if she alone were responsible for bringing them together. It was yet one more moment that she could wish would go on forever.

They bantered and laughed. The Captain called for sweet and sticky liqueurs to go with their coffee. He had the waiter bring him a pencil and some paper so that he could work out what the potential profit might be on forty cottages, plus the bar receipts and the dining-room profits. His mathematics were awful; Carol Anne had to take the pencil and do his sums for him. Then Robert wanted to sketch out his idea for an improved cottage, and he bent his head close to hers while he showed her his designs.

The Captain called for more coffee, more liqueurs, more pencils and paper. They all designed cottages. For a moment even the waiter got into the act after he'd poured the coffees, showing the Captain where a built-in patio table should go in case the guests wanted breakfast served out there.

And then they all had to figure out costs, and man-hours required to erect the cottages, and add them all up. Which of course turned the conversation toward Carol Anne's scheme for "The World's Greatest Antique Auction, Right Here in Mandeville." Both the men immediately began calculating which other house in the valley might have older furniture than the manor house, but neither would agree with the other.

But it was all argued about in fun; there was no longer any bitterness between the men, and no longer any need for Carol Anne to feel timid in front of Robert. Perhaps it was the wine—she'd finally got to taste the Australian wine Robert had ordered yesterday—perhaps it was the liqueurs on top of the wine, but whatever it was, she knew she loved both these men. One she loved because he was the dearest old man in the world. The other because . . . simply because he was Robert Innes, who was so happy now, and who wasn't worried anymore about the grand and expensive scheme for a hotel that his father wanted to put into effect.

At last they were full with coffee and food. Nobody wanted any more liqueur. Carol Anne felt her head spinning once in a while. They all got up as if with one thought and wandered out onto the veranda. The cool night air felt heavenly on her face. There was a three-quarter moon, low in the sky, yellow and near. All three stood there looking at it; then the Captain found a chair and sighed as he sat down.

"Think I'll just sit here, have a nightcap, and stare at the moon," he announced in a contented voice.

Robert looked at Carol Anne. He wasn't smiling. His eyes were deep and dark; she could look way down into his soul through them. They transfixed her.

"Feel like going for a walk?" he asked softly.

They walked through the gardens in silence, not touching, each lost in thought but both electrically aware of the other's presence. The night was comfortably cool, but Carol Anne could sense the warmth of Robert's body at her side.

125

The pretty lanterns were gone from the ornamental garden; only one tall and lonely lamp provided attraction for the moths, but the moon outshone it by far, calling to the more adventurous of the insects; they could see them flitting bravely skyward, trying to reach her enticing light. Carol Anne shivered involuntarily once, then shook her head to settle back her hair.

They strolled, still in silence, to the deserted floodlit pool, as still as translucent marble beneath their feet. Then, without either of them suggesting it, they walked away from the pool, their steps leading them to Find-your-man Hill. Carol Anne's heart was beating higher in her breast. Again she shook her head to settle her hair, which a newly awakened breeze was investigating with delicate fingers.

"That's nice," he said softly.

"What is?" She was puzzled.

"When you shake your hair back, the way you do. I like that," and he laughed very softly after he'd said it. "You'll never believe what it reminds me of."

They were walking more slowly now, up toward Find-your-man's scented bower. Carol Anne could feel a pull from the pretty place, drawing her nearer. Could he feel it too?

"What does it remind you of?" she asked, her voice as low as his own. She had to speak softly to keep her voice under control. Why was it so hard to keep it from trembling?

"Tiger," he said musingly.

"I remind you of a horse?" It was her turn to laugh. But he hurried to explain.

"No, no. Not of a horse. But of Tiger. He tosses his head a bit like you do sometimes. And when he does, I know he's getting wicked ideas in it." He bent to peer into Carol Anne's face, shadowy in the moonlight. She caught a glimpse of his own before averting her eyes. Somehow it had been too earth-shaking to do more than cast that swift glance. Had she looked hard into his eyes, the world would have ended and nature would have needed to start a new one, where everything was changed, and she didn't know if she wanted that, yet.

She tried to make her voice light. "Do you think I've got wicked ideas like Tiger, just because I shake my head?" and as she said it she had an almost uncontrollable impulse to shake her hair back again. The breeze was teasing it again. But she held herself in check.

For a few paces he was silent; then he chuckled. "I don't know about you, but as for me . . ."

She glanced at him again, a sudden smile at the edge of her lips. "It gives you wicked ideas? I'd better not do it, then." But the breeze had lifted her hair so that she had to shake it back into place.

He didn't say anything, nor did he laugh, which might have broken the rising, exciting tension. Instead he looked at her after she had done it, but she kept her own eyes averted. Her heart was pounding and her mind was a jumble of whirling thoughts. Desperately she sought among them for something safe and banal to say, anything that might put off the moment which she felt so strongly was approaching. Her entire being wanted that moment to arrive, but her mind tried to argue "No." It would be wrong. She had to leave the island, while Robert had to stay. His future and hers followed different paths. The fact that, here and now, when their paths had crossed for just a moment, seemed so right and good made no difference; their futures would separate soon and she didn't want either of them to be burdened with bitter memories merely because she had allowed one long and lovely moment to exist. But she could think of nothing to say, and unconsciously she shook her head again.

They stopped on the crest of the hill with the moon directly ahead of them, bathing the far valley in mystery, while the oddly nostalgic scent of frangiapani rose to meet their tingling senses. She felt his hand touch her own and found herself being led to the stone bench in the flower-scented arbor at the top of Find-your-man Hill. In a daze of delight she let him lead her there, and sat down beside him.

Instinctively, despairingly, she turned to face him, looking into his eyes. She felt his hands grip her arms tightly, as if he was trying to control himself by doing so, and then his eager lips were over hers and she closed her eyes in grateful surrender. She was home at last. His hands left her arms and came around her, for such a strange weakness came over her that she would have fallen had he not done so, and her own arms reached up, encircling his neck, pulling him to her so that she could return his kiss, pressing against him in glorious abandon, living for a moment in eternity.

But suddenly there was an urgency in his grasp. Robert's lips sought hers with a demanding need. And at first she responded, as eager as he himself. She felt herself borne down, his left arm cradling her head, his right hand on her breast, his face buried in the hollow of her neck.

He groaned aloud, and the sound brought Carol Anne to her senses.

"Robert. No. Please, Robert!" She struggled in his grasp, turning her face away from his.

His grip relaxed and she wriggled free, her mind whirling except for one small place where it was as icy calm as a frozen lake. She stood up, pushing her hair back with both hands.

"I'm cold. We should go back inside. The Captain will be wondering about us." The icy part of her mind was slowly spreading. But the hot, exultant part of her gave way reluctantly. It was all she could do to stand there and watch him; one word from him would have seen her fling herself back into his embrace.

But he spoke no word. Instead he sat up, looking at her for a moment standing before him, the light of the moon behind her; then he got to his feet.

They walked a few paces side by side, and he took her hand. The gesture said all that was in his mind. She held it tight, comforting him, pleading with her grasp for him to understand her, to forgive her, to forget her, to remember only that so very soon their ways must part forever, and that no memories should exist to form scars over their souls, once they were apart.

He left her at the steps into the manor house. The Captain had already gone inside, so they were alone except for the moths making shadows against the tall lamp lighting the driveway. He held her hand in his right until they reached the steps, and before he let go he turned her to him, still holding her hand, and slowly bent to give her one chaste kiss on the lips before turning away, still without a word, and going to his cottage.

Carol Anne stood like a statue, watching him go, her mind at long last settling down, the thoughts beginning to make sense.

Why had he kissed her like that, on Find-your-man Hill? What did he think of her now? And how could he face Cathy after tonight? Wasn't he in love with Cathy after all? A sudden surge of hope spread through her, but she quickly dampened it down at once. No, she told herself. You are leaving soon. This is not your life.

Stinging tears came to her eyes. Blindly she stumbled up the steps into the old house.

Next morning as Carol Anne was finishing breakfast on the veranda Robert mounted the creaking steps to join her. He stood looking down on her, giving her a smile that made her heart race. She could see that her apprehension about how he would treat her in the light of day was unfounded.

"Good morning, Carol Anne. I thought I'd stay home today and let the work tend to itself. Mind if I join you for a cup of coffee?" He took a chair, waiting until the waiter had poured his cup full from the two silver jugs.

"I've been thinking about that idea of yours. About the old furniture. Perhaps it wouldn't be a bad idea to go

129

through the rooms and see what there is"—he gestured at the courtyard beyond the veranda—"especially as it's raining."

Carol Anne hadn't even noticed it was raining. She had awakened that morning in a delicious daze, her mind still full of the events of the night before. She didn't hear a word that Charlene said; she didn't even remember getting dressed.

She did remember going out onto the little balcony to smile at the newborn day, but she didn't recall that it had been raining. Instead it seemed that never had the sky been so blue; never had the birds sung more sweetly than they did that morning. It had seemed like the best and most wonderful morning in the best and most beautiful of worlds. She even remembered turning to Charlene and saying so: "Charlene? Isn't today just gorgeous?" And Charlene had laughed aloud and continued making the bed, and it had all been so wonderfully natural and at the same time so marvelous.

Then when she came downstairs and saw that the green lizard was back under the rafters with his yellow throat puffed out, waiting for his own breakfast, she'd said, "Hello, little green lizard, isn't it a beautiful morning?" but of course the tiny lizard hadn't answered. So she tossed it a bread crumb, startling it away so that she'd laughed aloud and the waiter came over to see if she wanted anything.

"Oh, no," she told him. "But isn't it a beautiful day?" And the waiter had gone away smiling, but looking puzzled. Now here was Robert pointing out something which should have been obvious to her from the moment she got up: Undeniably it was raining; not a heavy rain—more of a liquid mist—but rain all the same. How could she have missed noticing it?

Robert followed her astounded gaze. "This sort of rain doesn't last very long," he apologized. "It's generally over by midday, so I wouldn't worry. Anyway, there's no point in traipsing through the fields in a rain like this, so I thought I'd kill two birds with one stone and look through the house. That is if you don't mind me tagging along?"

What was this? This was a new Robert entirely. Or was he mocking her? She could never tell. Yet, after last night, perhaps he had changed; perhaps he was seriously asking if she minded having him along—as if that was possible— but even so he was quite different from the brusque and dominant Robert who was more likely to give her orders than to ask for her permission about anything. She didn't quite know how to take him.

They started with the ground floor: the bar, a large drawing room, a surprising little music room with a baby grand piano in it, some rooms which Robert said were offices and utility rooms, and then the dining room. As he showed her around, Robert began to adopt a proprietary attitude, as if he was starting to understand what his father had accomplished with the old house. But he kept strictly to the matter at hand; he never mentioned last night. Carol Anne didn't want to be the first to bring the subject up, so little by little it became as if it had never happened. What a strange man Robert was. Carol Anne just didn't know what to make of him. Was he ashamed of last night? Was he playing games with her?

Well, if he didn't want to mention it, neither would she. Determinedly she shut her mind to the question.

They went from the dining room through a serving door into a large kitchen, where there were modern stainless-steel cabinets with glass fronts, sinks and stoves and dishwashing equipment as up-to-date as anything in Toronto. Carol Anne turned to Robert with her eyebrows raised.

Robert laughed. "Well, I'll admit I had a heart attack when I saw the bill, but I imagine we'll be needing it now. That Dino character designed it."

"You could feed an army from here!"

"Might have to, if your idea about the cottages comes true. Might be hundreds here if we have that antique sale of yours."

Inwardly she was pleased that Robert had used the word "antiques." He'd stopped thinking in terms of selling off his own furniture, so that was another hurdle overcome. Strange, though, how people changed when they put different labels to their thoughts.

They mounted the grand staircase after they left the kitchen, off to inspect the upstairs rooms. Carol Anne always felt queenly on those stairs.

For the first time sine she'd come to the manor house Carol Anne walked past the door to her own room, which was close to the head of the stairs, and along the wide corridor. At once she began to realize just how enormous the manor house was. Robert showed her room after room. Over the years some attempt had been made to give each room its own individuality: One room had green wallpaper, and green curtains, with touches of green about the furniture. Presumably someone had intended it to be the Green Room. The next room seemed to be the Rose Room, and was quite pretty. Other rooms were not. The Blue Room in particular was a disaster, to Carol Anne's taste. She itched to change it around.

But all rooms had certain things in common. Each had the tall ceilings and spacious dimensions of her own room, and all the rooms were filled to overflowing—stuffed was the word that came into her mind—with far too many pieces of furniture. And all the furniture was old, at least. And much of it was beautiful. It was an antique mine. The new cottages were as good as paid for.

She turned to Robert after seeing the eighth or ninth room and threw her arms wide.

"Be honest, now. Don't you really feel there's just far too much furniture in the manor house?"

"Now that I look at it your way, I expect I do. It had just never crossed my mind before. But it's true, we could get rid of half the stuff in those rooms and never miss it, never even know it was gone."

She felt like hugging him.

"Can I write to Mr. Roxlet so that he can contact the

auctioneer right away? There's a tremendous amount of work to be done before the actual sale."

"I don't see why not. I suppose we're all committed to this venture now, so go ahead." He laughed again, catching some of her enthusiasm. "So you'd better start the ball rolling; I'm quite sure neither the Captain nor I would know how to go about it, nor even where to start. So go ahead."

They went downstairs at last via the back stairway at the far end of the hallway. It descended into a room she hadn't seen so far. A large billiard table took up most of it, and there were many comfortable chairs all around the table. It was very much a man's room, without any feminine touches.

She turned to Robert, smiling impishly. "Now, don't tell me Dino di Cavour designed this room too?"

"No." Robert grinned back. "This room has been like this since the eighteen-nineties; nearly a hundred years. My own great-grandfather had it installed."

"I'm glad he did; it will certainly come in handy on rainy days. Can you get to this room without coming down the stairs?"

"Through here. Just follow me." He led the way through a door into a long hallway, at the end of which was another door leading them to the foot of the grand staircase.

"Well? What did you think of it? That's the whole house, unless you'd like to see the attic."

Carol Anne's eyes lit up. "Is there an attic too?"

"The length and width of the house; you could play a game of football up there, except that it's jammed full of junk." But Carol Anne had seized his hand and was already dragging him up the stairs.

"Where is it? I've got to see it. How do we get there?"

"What on earth for?"

"Because it could be a gold mine," she gasped. "That junk you mentioned could very well be priceless."

Robert had to laugh. "Don't be silly, it's really junk; it's

133

just things that were too good to throw out but weren't worth having in the house." They reached the head of the stairs. "Anyway, it's fearfully dusty up there. You'll get filthy in no time."

Carol Anne stopped short. They were close to her room.

"Wait a minute, then." She ran inside her room and looked on her bed. Just as she thought they would be, there were her jeans and the shirt she'd worn yesterday to go riding, now freshly washed and ironed. She closed the door, stripped off her dress, threw it on the bed and pulled on her jeans.

"Oh, no!" she cried, horrified.

Then immediately she burst out laughing.

"Charlene, how could you!" Charlene had starched her jeans. She scooped the white shirt off the bed. It too was starched.

But she pulled it on, tucked it into her jeans, looked in the cupboard and found her boots, dragging them on too, then walked to the door, crackling like wrapping paper.

Robert was still there in the hall, right where she'd left him.

"Now," she announced, "let's go up into that dusty old attic and see what we can see."

The door to the attic, at the top of a steep and narrow flight of stairs, hadn't been opened for years. But it was not locked, and gave way after Robert put his shoulder to it and heaved. He stepped through, fumbled on the wall, found a light switch and beckoned Carol Anne through.

"Watch out for spiderwebs," he cautioned. "Some of the blighters bite, you know."

"Ugh!" said Carol Anne, shivering. She wished she'd found a scarf to wear as a bandana.

"Hello!" said Robert. "Look what I've found. Hope it works." He picked up a long flashlight from the floor, tried it and from it came a feeble yellow light. "That's luck." He grinned.

Carol Anne stared around her. Half a dozen dim and

dusty bulbs cast an eerie light on mounds and piles of dust-covered objects. At each end of the attic were grimy windows so thick with dust that very little sunlight came through. Robert handed her the flashlight. "Here, perhaps you'd better have this."

She accepted it gratefully, directing the faint beam around her. The mounds of dust-covered objects now became piles of furniture. Her eyes widened.

"It *is* gold mine," she breathed, "I'm sure of it."

"Aha! Here's my ancestor's sea chest; I knew it was up here somewhere. It must have been stuffed with doubloons and pieces of eight once." Carol Anne directed the beam at the heavy-looking black wooden chest Robert had found. It had silver corner pieces and a brass hasp.

"That you don't sell," she said positively. "That should be cleaned up and polished, and set somewhere in the bar with a plaque on it telling whose it was and how it came here." She shone the light on a graceful dressing table with a cracked mirror, studying it.

"My great-great-grandmother's, I think. She came from England and brought a lot of furniture with her, back in the eighteen-fifties. This looks like something of hers. But it's got a cracked mirror, so who'd want it now?"

Carol Anne laughed aloud, shaking her head. "Oh, you've got a lot to learn about the antique business," she warned him.

She stepped gingerly forward, shining the light from side to side. "Everything in here must be a hundred years old."

"Oh, at least that. My mother was supposed to have cleaned a lot of things out of the downstairs rooms right after she married my father, and had them all stored up here. That was thirty-five years ago, and these things were old then."

"I'd like to have met your mother."

"I wish you could have met her too. She was a lovely lady. I think you two would have liked each other."

Odd, thought Carol Anne, just a while ago I was

135

wondering how Mom would get along with Robert. And now it's plain he's been wondering how I would have got along with *his* mother. Musing over the thought, she stepped forward without watching where she was going.

"Watch out!" Robert's arms were suddenly about her, pulling her back. Wide-eyed, she saw that she had been about to walk into a huge spiderweb, spun with care and skill across the aisle along which she was walking. But the thought of the web and the monstrous spider waiting in its center vanished at the realization that Robert hadn't let go of her now that she was out of danger. Her heart was racing. Was it from fright? Or was it something else? She turned in Robert's arms, looking at his face.

"Some of those things bite," he said huskily. "They can be very nasty." But he still didn't take his arms from around her. She could feel his arms trembling slightly. Or was it she herself who was trembling? Perhaps it was both of them?

"Thank you," she said simply. "I don't want to be bitten; not by anything, but especially spiders."

Both his arms were around her. She could feel the very faintest pressure from them, drawing her closer to him. His face was shadowed; she could not see his expression. Her arms were at her sides, held there despite an almost overpowering need to drop the flashlight and fling them around Robert's neck. But she did restrain herself. The knowledge that in a few days she would be gone from here acted like a wall in her mind, one that her inclinations couldn't climb over.

Slowly his arms relaxed their hold around her, until at last he stood clear. She still could not see his face, so she had no idea what his expression might be. She waited for him to speak.

"It's stopped raining, I think. The sun's coming out." He pointed briefly. She looked at the window and saw bright sunshine coming through; dust motes whirled in the sunbeams.

136

"Have you seen all you want to see? Because I'd better be getting off to work," he added. His voice was light and matter-of-fact, as if nothing had happened, as if he was trying to restore their relationship to what it had appeared to be on the surface; the owner of a house showing an interested guest around. Tears stung the back of Carol Anne's eyes. For a fleeting second she remembered last night with Robert on Find-your-man Hill. But that was an accident, she told herself; it was only the almost inevitable result of too many drinks at dinner and too big a moon in the sky. Robert himself obviously thought so too. Why else had he made no reference to it? None at all! It was as if it had never happened.

Right, she determined; if that's the way it is to be, then that's the way it will be. Her own voice was matter-of-fact when she spoke.

"That's true," she admitted. "Men must work, and women must weep, so they say." Then she laughed, to show him there was no hidden meaning in what she'd said. But she knew there was.

She gave him back the flashlight. "The little bit I've seen up here," she told him, "shows me that there are enough antiques right inside this house for a successful auction. You don't need to get anything from the other houses. In fact, you could flood the market if they have as much inside them as the manor house does." Her voice was businesslike and purposeful; she made it that way deliberately, so as to set his mind at ease about their relationship. She was trying by the tone of her voice to let him know that she was prepared to consider what had happened between them as nothing more than a chance encounter, if that was the way he wanted it. And that he needn't worry that she'd try to take advantage of it.

"So now, you've got to get to work, and I've got dozens of notes I have to write down for Mr. Roxlet." She waited for him to make the next move.

"Carol Anne . . ." he began, not moving, his voice somehow unsure—she'd never heard it sound like this before. But he didn't say anything else. Finally she had to speak.

"Yes?"

"You're quite right," he announced, as if he'd made a decision. "We've both got work to do." Turning, he led the way to the door.

It was still quite a while before lunch by the time Carol Anne got showered and changed, her mind filled with puzzles that she couldn't unravel. So she took Mr. Roxlet's questionnaire and forced herself to fill it out, making long handwritten notes to flesh out sections that the questionnaire didn't cover adequately. But after a while she was stuck; nowhere on the questionnaire was there any place that indicated exactly what sort of hotel the manor house would be.

And then another thought struck her. The manor house! She turned to the front part of the questionnaire; The Innes Estate Hotel, it said. She looked at it for a moment, then thoughtfully crossed it out. Above it she wrote: The Manor House Hotel.

That was more like it. The Manor House Hotel. That was what best described this new venture. Because it certainly wasn't a luxury hotel, yet neither was it a simple guest house. It was . . . well, just what it was: unique. The Manor House of Mandeville, a place where people could rent a cottage for a month or a season, and where they could live the life of well-to-do Jamaican country people, seeing the local life just the way it was, without pretense or sham. A good life, settled, ancient, but solid and good. Something that just wasn't available in Toronto or New York or London—or even Paris or Rome, she added, thinking of Dino and Cathy McKinnon. A place where a family could relax, if they could afford it, and soak up the old, worthwhile values and way of life.

The Manor House.

She felt so excited about the new name and concept that

138

she simply had to go and find the Captain and tell him about it.

He wasn't downstairs on the veranda, nor in the bar. But the barman knew where he was.

"He's in his office, miss." He gave her directions to find him.

It was a small room, one that she'd missed on this morning's tour of all the large rooms. It was cluttered and piled with books and ledgers on shelves, and spilled over onto the big oak desk behind which the Captain was sitting. Carol Anne's eyes lit up at the sight of all the account books; a couple of days with them and an adding machine and she'd know every secret of the manor house, the estate, properties. There was an open ledger on the desk in front of the Captain.

"Ah. So you ran me to earth, eh? Little job I have to attend to, won't take me long. Have to do the books now, you see. Hateful job, but has to be done. My good lady did it before she left me, and now it's my job. Terrible business. Bloody bore, in fact."

"Bookkeeping's not boring," Carol Anne blurted out indignantly, then blushed. She sat in the seat in front of the desk, hoping to hide her confusion. "You see," she explained, "I used to be a bookkeeper before I transferred over and became a travel agent. In fact, I was the head bookkeeper at the Roxlet Travel Agency. I liked book-keeping; it's all so commonsensical and neat."

"My beloved was like that too," cried the Captain, seemingly astonished. "Must be some sort of instinct the ladies have. Must say it's all beyond me, truly."

"I'd like to help you," ventured Carol Anne, her eyes gleaming again at the thought of poking through those ledgers and accounts. She was suddenly sure they contained the clue to the reason Robert's farms weren't paying off.

"Couldn't think of it." The old man smiled, closing the ledger he'd been working on. "Wouldn't dream of imposing on you like that. But tell me, what brings you in here so full of excitement?"

"The Manor House Hotel!" Carol Anne told him about the name change, and how it would work better for the hotel, speaking rapidly in her excitement. "And it has a more solid, homelike sound to it, too," she ended.

He was as pleased as she was. "And I don't mind guessing that Robert will like it too. He's been so dead set against the Innes estate being turned into a hotel. But he can't object to an entirely new hotel called the Manor House, can he?"

He rubbed his hands together in delight, then pushed himself upright. "You're full of good ideas, m'dear; a perpetual spring of them. So many that I simply must escort you in to lunch and stay with you, in case you come up with another one."

She took his arm as they left the office. "Captain Innes, would you believe me if I told you I haven't been a travel agent very long?"

"My dear, I'd believe you if you told me you hadn't been anything at all very long. You're quite young, you know. You couldn't have been a travel agent longer than a year or two."

"Would you believe one month?"

"Ha!" the Captain exploded in laughter, stopping to look her over. "One month you say? Ha! At this rate you'll have bought out Mr. Roxlet by the time you've been an agent a year. Ha!" He shook with glee as they marched along. But then he stopped and faced her. "M'dear, if you're worried that anyone may hold that against you, then don't. I, for one, would give you the most glowing recommendation, if asked. Truly I would. You've done absolute wonders."

Relieved of her small burden of guilt, Carol Anne spilled out the whole story over lunch, telling him how she felt like such a fraud because Robert imagined she was a world traveler.

"I've never been to Paris or Rome," she said unhappily.

"I know all about the hotels there, and the sights, and how to get there and where the airports are, but I've never been there."

"Don't you worry, m'dear. You'll go there. All in good time."

"But it isn't that. It's, well, Robert seems to think I go gadabouting all over the world at the drop of a hat; everyone thinks so—even people like Dino de Cavour. And I haven't. Lots of travel agents stay close to the office. When I get back in a day or two, it might be a year before I go anywhere again."

"You can't go back," began the Captain indignantly. Then he realized what he was saying, and rephrased it. "At least, not until Sunday's flight at the earliest."

"But by then I'll have been here a whole week."

"I'll telephone your Mr. Roxlet after lunch and tell him you're quite indispensable to me just now. If he argues, I'll tell him you've done so much for us that you deserve a holiday."

Carol Anne laughed, then remembered that Mr. Roxlet *did* say she could take a few days off. "This whole week has been a holiday, but I'm certain Mr. Roxlet won't mind."

"Even so. I'll talk the blighter into it. Trust me."

Chapter Eight

Carol Anne escaped to her room after lunch with the feeling that she absolutely had to be alone. She'd taken care to eat sparingly this time, so she wasn't so stuffed that she would need a nap to overcome the feeling. She needed time to think.

While she sat for those moments in the Captain's office she'd been able to see that the page in the ledger he was working on wasn't neat. It had crossed-out entries on it, and lines presumably leading certain entries into other columns. It looked dreadful. Amateurish and clumsy. It looked more like a very rough worksheet than a finished page in a ledger. But she'd had the feeling that this was, in fact, the finished page. Which meant that it was bound to be filled with errors; which meant that very likely the errors in there could account for Robert's farms not making any money. She itched to get at those books.

Because, how *could* Robert's farms not make money! Doug McKinnon obviously made money off his land; she'd asked in a roundabout way what size the McKinnon holdings might be, at lunchtime, and the Captain had said they were roughly the same size as the Innes estate. McKinnon's land couldn't be any better; he certainly couldn't work any harder than Robert. And she had seen with her own eyes how well-run and orderly Robert's farms were. So the problem had to be financial.

The Captain knew it, and was taking his own steps to solve it; because the farms needed money, he was venturing into the hotel business, in hopes of making enough profit to keep the farms going. But that wasn't the correct solution. Certainly, the way things were going, the hotel would be a success. Inevitably it would make money, if everyone was careful at the start. But she couldn't imagine Robert being satisfied to have his father's hotel support his farms. It would shame him to death.

She'd been lying on the bed with a furrowed brow. This wouldn't do. She leaped up and found her swimsuit. She could think just as well by the side of the pool, and get a tan into the bargain.

She hurried over to the pool, her terry-cloth robe almost streaming behind her because she was in such a rush. Somehow she felt sure that all the pieces she needed to solve this puzzle were already in her head, and all she needed to do was lie somewhere quietly so that the pieces could stop whirling around, and would settle down into an orderly pattern so that she could see at last what they said.

She slowed down. There were people at the pool. She could hear them even before she got to where the path led through the hedge; splashing sounds and happy laughter, the bong-bong-bong of the diving board when somebody jumped off it. She was tempted to go back to her room. Then curiosity overcame her. Who were these people? She walked on again.

There were half a dozen of them or so; some of the Mandeville crowd. They all shouted greetings when she appeared.

She waved back, squinting through her sunglasses, trying to remember names and put them to faces. Naturally, now that the place was a hotel, there would be guests and visitors at the pool; she should have realized that. And then she saw Cathy McKinnon. Her heart stopped for one moment.

Cathy McKinnon had the kind of figure that looked simply stunning in a bikini. Not just good—stunning. She wore a white one. Her lovely golden hair was piled up on top of her head and knotted into a bun, just the way Carol Anne had done her own hair the night of the party. Copycat, thought Carol Anne ungraciously. Her tan was perfect, smooth and golden and even; Carol Anne felt sure it didn't end where her bikini began but, continued all over, just as smoothly and evenly. She must use sunlamps, she told herself. Either that or . . . she closed her mind to the unkind thought.

She was almost uncivilizedly delighted to notice that Cathy McKinnon's vaccination mark was somewhat more pronounced than it should be, a visible round scar on the upper part of her lovely left leg. Then she rebuked herself. Why should she be jealous if Cathy McKinnon was beautiful? What business was it of hers? Hadn't she gone all through that yesterday while lying in the bathtub? But then she remembered last night, after dinner, on Find-your-man Hill with Robert. She allowed herself to hate Cathy McKinnon a little bit.

It all went through her head in the minute between noticing Cathy standing at the side of the pool and seeing her wave to her, beckoning her over. What could Cathy want with her?

She walked around the pool toward Cathy, who was the center of a group of young men and one other girl. The men were charming, one leaping to his feet to get her a deck chair, another ready to rush to the bar the moment she decided what she wanted to drink. There were introductions all around, and smiles, yet there was an undercurrent that Carol Anne felt, flowing from Cathy McKinnon, which disturbed her.

"I've been so wanting to meet you," Cathy was saying. "Robert talks so much about you. Only this morning he was telling me about some simply marvelous idea you have for an auction sale." Cathy had a marked British accent. She gave the word "idea" three distinct syllables.

144

Carol Anne spread her robe over the back of the deck chair and sat down. So, she'd met Robert this morning? This girl sure got around.

"And he's told me so much about you, too. You won a tennis cup together."

"Oh, dear me, that little mixed-doubles thing? I'd forgotten all about it. But it's true, Robert and I are *quite* close."

Was this a warning of some sort? Carol Anne studied Cathy's face through her sunglasses. But Cathy was wearing sunglasses too, so she couldn't make out her eyes.

Young Harry, who'd gone to get Carol Anne her drink, came back with it, setting it before her and dragging up a chair. He was the same boy who'd danced so many dances with her a few nights ago. Harry was a lively, bright-eyed boy of about her own age, but Carol Anne felt ages older than he was.

"You've no idea what excitement you've brought to Mandeville," he assured Carol Anne. He had perfect teeth and a lovely smile. "There were a lot who were betting against the Captain's hotel idea, but it seems you're going to put it on the map, so everyone's changing their minds."

"I'm glad to hear that. It's going to be a lovely hotel. People will come from all over the world and stay for months. They'll join in the fun, they'll get to know you, and you can get to know them if you feel inclined."

"It will certainly set sleepy old Mandeville on its ear, let me tell you. Why, Fred Taylor's even thinking of redecorating his old pub—isn't he, Cathy?"

"She wouldn't know who Fred Taylor is, Harry. She's only been here a day or two." Cathy got two syllables out of "here."

"Oh, of course. Fred runs a pub; a fairly popular watering hole, in fact. But it's sort of seedy. Now he's hoping to attract some of the Captain's guests over for the evening, when they're here, so he's spending a few bob on paint. And he's not the only one. Lots of stores and bars

145

and eating houses are sprucing up. You've no idea of all the excitement."

"I'm just delighted to hear it." And she was. She'd been so busy with the specific problems of the hotel itself that she'd spared no time to consider the effect of the hotel on the local community. Now she realized she'd need to make a note of the possibilities of Mandeville as an added attraction for guests of the manor house hotel.

"Even the country people are getting involved," Harry went on. "They've always made straw hats and things for the Victoria Market in Kingston, where the cruise ships pull in. But now there's talk of opening an arts-and-crafts market right in Mandeville."

"Harry? Would you be a dear and get me a drink? A gin and tonic would be nice."

"Sure, Cathy," and obliging Harry was on his feet and off to the bar like a trained puppy after a ball, delighted with his task. Cathy and Carol Anne were alone now. The others at the table had gone into the pool and were splashing and laughing, chasing each other.

"I'm rather pleased your work is going so well," Cathy said. "I suppose you'll be leaving soon?"

"The Captain has asked me to stay on for a few more days, but by Sunday I suppose I'll be back in Toronto."

"Is Toronto your home? How sad for you."

Carol Anne's eyes widened. Had she heard right?

"I've never been there, of course, but I've passed through Toronto en route to more interesting places," Cathy continued. "I imagine you take every opportunity you can to get away from it?"

How dare this woman insult her hometown? Then suddenly Carol Anne realized that Cathy was deliberately trying to bait her, trying to get her so angry she'd say something stupid. She took a slow, deep breath, smiling at Cathy, calming herself.

"I rather like your part of the world," she answered at last, waving a hand to encompass the valley. "It was really lovely here, until you came back, of course."

146

Cathy laughed in genuine delight. "Oh? A sense of humor? How nice. So seldom to be found in a Canadian. But of course you've traveled, so that would explain it. Travel *is* so educational, don't you think?"

Carol Anne agreed, sensing a trap. But Harry came back with the drink before Cathy could spring it. She accepted the gin and tonic regally, letting Harry put it on the table for her, not lifting a hand until he had. Carol Anne was trying to gather her wits about her. What had Cathy found out to make her so testy? Why was she picking on her like this?

Harry didn't stay long. Someone called him from the water, and off he went, diving cleanly from the side, surfacing under another young man, whom he tipped over with a roar and a splash.

Cathy watched him go, visibly amused.

"Yes, it is nice to be home at last," she mused. "Nice to see all the old friends. I think I'll stay home, at least for a while, now that I'm here." She turned her gaze back to Carol Anne. "They do say home is where the heart is. Where is your heart, dear?"

Carol Anne laughed and didn't answer. So Cathy continued.

"I hope it isn't with Robert Innes, at least. Such a handsome hunk of man. So . . . virile, don't you think? It would be easy to forgive any girl who fell for him, because any girl in her right mind would, wouldn't she? Yes, it would be very easy to forgive a girl for that, as long as she was far away from him and likely to stay there." She laughed gently. "Far, far away," she insisted.

At last it was clear. Somehow, probably because she'd probed it out of Robert, Cathy had managed to hear, or guess, about last night on Find-your-man Hill. She was giving her a warning that she considered Robert Innes her own, and that Carol Anne should stay away.

Resentment flooded through her. She was about to retort sharply when Cathy spoke again.

"Robert told me he's planning a going-away party for

147

you on Saturday night. Perhaps he'll choose the same night to announce our engagement—I haven't quite decided if that would be the right moment or not, so of course you mustn't mention it to anyone, dear; a girl likes to make her own mind up about such things, don't you think?"

Engaged? To Robert? Her heart sank out of sight.

But, what could be more natural? He and Cathy were longtime friends, partners in sports of various kinds—remembrance of last night on Find-your-man Hill crept into her mind.

But how could he be planning to get engaged and take her to Find-your-man Hill at the same time? Was he some sort of louse? But he couldn't be. Not Robert. It just wasn't his style. And anyway, she had known last night that it had been no casual, spur-of-the-moment relationship for him, just as it wasn't for her. Cathy must be lying. She stared at her, pushing her sunglasses up onto her hair to see her better. Cathy laughed and pushed her own glasses up. She had luminous green eyes, scornful and arrogant eyes that twinkled at Carol Anne in unconcealed victory. Carol Anne put her glasses back on and lay back on the deck chair, staring up at the sky.

Well, if what Cathy said was true, then Cathy had been quite civilized in the way she'd acted, giving her a warning, but not being downright rude and telling her to keep her hands off. Carol Anne began to sense a tiny bit of admiration for Cathy.

Resolutely she squashed the feeling flat. Cathy wasn't going to win so easily; there were still more days left before she had to leave for home, and anything could happen.

But she knew she'd lost, even as she tried to plan to win. Cathy was more beautiful, more talented, better educated, even a better rider, certainly a better sportswoman, and men liked sports. She had known Robert for years too, and could exercise the familiarity of long

148

friendship. She was going to stay here, while Carol Anne would have to leave. Cathy could afford to dress better, to pay to go places. . . .

There it was again, the fact that Cathy had money, yet her father didn't have. Where did she get her money from?

"Where will you go on your honeymoon?" Carol Anne asked without turning to look at Cathy. Cathy laughed softly, a note of triumph in her voice. So, she figures she's got me beaten, Carol Anne mused. Well, let her. Let's see what happens.

"Oh . . . Istanbul is nice at this time of the year. But so is Marrakesh—it's hard to say."

"I've a feeling Robert wouldn't be able to afford a long trip overseas, but I wouldn't know."

"Robert will be able to afford anything he likes, now that the hotel venture looks to be so successful."

"Perhaps so, but the hotel won't make a profit in its first season. Are you planning to wait until next year before you get married?"

"Heavens no. We'll be married as soon as we feel like it. And once the hotel starts to operate, there'll be a dozen people waiting in line to lend Robert all he needs, whenever he wants it." Cathy laughed again. "In any case, money is not the problem you may think. I've got plenty for both of us for now, and Daddy has plenty more if that fails."

Carol Anne tensed. She deliberately controlled her breathing; for a moment back there she'd almost gasped at the news. So, not only Cathy had money, but her father had "plenty more if that fails," so where was the truth in this story that none of the farmers in this valley was making ends meet? Now she had proof that Doug McKinnon at least was making plenty. And he was the one who managed the farm cooperative. He must be cheating everyone in the co-op. But how?

"The Captain tells me you were born in Uganda,"

149

Carol Anne said at last, in what she hoped was a conversational tone despite her racing heart. "That must have been exciting for you."

"Hmmmm. 'Exciting' is hardly the appropriate word. 'Frightening' would be more like it. I was only a teenage girl, of course, when we left—hardly younger than you are now—but I distinctly recall being terrified. Of course it was simply darling before that awful Amin took over." She seemed to fall into a reverie. Carol Anne risked a peek. Cathy was staring up into the vaulted sky, her glasses still on her hair. From the corner of her eye she caught Carol Anne's glance.

"Why are you so interested in Uganda?"

"Oh. I've never been there. I imagine it must have been very like it is here now. I don't know. I just don't want to talk about Robert," she lied, turning her head again and closing her eyes. In a moment she could hear Cathy settling back into her chair again.

"That's very thoughtful of you," Cathy said, then was silent.

Carol Anne opened her eyes again. Far overhead in the depths of heaven a high-flying jet was making a white streak across the otherwise startlingly blue sky. She tried to make out the airplane itself, but could only see a white dot.

"You mustn't lie too long in the sun if you're not used to it," Cathy warned. "You can get an awful burn."

Carol Anne obediently rolled over onto her stomach. The back of the deck chair forced her chin too high, so she propped her folded arms under it. How was she going to find out where Cathy got her money? There was no way she planned to leave until she'd at least got a clue.

"It must be nice to have a private income," Carol Anne said softly, as if truly thinking how pleasant it might be. She kept her voice soft and ruminative. Cathy was lying back at ease in her deck chair with her eyes closed. And when she answered, it was only to make an unintelligible sound.

"Unhunh," she said sleepily.

Unhunh? Now, what could that mean? Carol Anne wondered. But, still in a sleepy voice, Cathy was speaking again.

"It's even nicer than you think, dear. Because I don't have to do any work at all—I probably wouldn't know how to anyway. My two partners do it all. I just collect dividends."

"Partners? Anyone I know?"

"Hardly, dear, unless you know my father."

"Yes, I've met your father. A very nice old gentleman, he seemed," Carol Anne said with a straight face, not meaning one word of it.

"You have?" Still in that sleepy hyponotized voice. "But I doubt you've met our senior partner; he never comes to Jamaica. . . ." She mumbled the last words as if half-asleep. Then her deck chair screeched as Cathy suddenly sat up. "Good heaven," she said, "I almost dropped off. Dangerous thing to do. Anyone could walk by and catch me with my mouth open. Well"—she got to her feet—"I'll be seeing you at dinner. Don't forget our little talk, dear, will you?"

And in a moment she was gone, striding like a young man, waving good-bye to all the people in the water.

Carol Anne left the pool soon after Cathy did, and changed in her room. She put on the jeans again, and went behind the manor house to the stables, stroking the nose of the gentle mare that had carried her home yesterday.

But horses have a very limited vocabulary, and a girl can't spend much time stroking even the most velvety nose without starting to wonder if life has more to offer, she decided.

She wanted to talk to someone. But who? And what did she want to tell them anyway? That she had lost Robert? But she'd never had him; last night was an interlude, that's all, and in any case she wasn't about to discuss last

151

night with anyone, not even her closest friend. Last night was private and precious. How had Cathy learned about it? Or had she learned? Had she only guessed, perhaps? She couldn't imagine Robert telling anyone, least of all a girl—especially Cathy McKinnon. No, she must have only guessed at something, and then she dropped a hint that she knew more than she did know.

Without thinking, simply because of her need to put into words what was troubling her, Carol Anne spoke aloud, stroking the horse's nose.

"I've got to leave here soon, and I want to stay. But I can't, you see, because I don't belong here. I have to go back up north to where I live." The mare pointed her ears at Carol Anne, thought better of it, and allowed one ear to point straight up. But the other one was obviously all attention. Carol Anne took heart.

"I've pretty well done what I was sent down to do. I can clean up the details as soon as I'm back. And anyway, Mr. Roxlet will want to handle the antique sale, and the advertising, and things like that. So I've done my job here. I can fill in the rest of the details on the form after dinner tonight, and then it's all done."

Now both ears were straight up. The horse looked bored.

"Do you know who's coming to dinner tonight?" she asked in a conspiratorial whisper. The mare moved back a pace, startled. Carol Anne put a finger to her lips. "A witch! A beautiful witch." Carol Anne dropped the hand from her lips,

It would be so nice to have someone to talk to, she thought as she left the stables. Who was there? Charlene? Ummm, no. Not Charlene. Her husband? Definitely not. The Captain?

He would listen. She knew he'd listen to her troubles; he was such a nice old man, and he'd said over and over that he depended on her just now, so surely he'd listen to her problems.

She stopped by the tennis courts. There were yellow-

152

painted benches on the courts so that spectators could watch the play. She went behind the high wire fence and sat down, leaning back against the wire. Even if the Captain would listen, what could she tell him? She stretched her feet out on the red-clay ground, pushed both hands deep into the pockets of her jeans and tried to think.

Carol Anne Todd, she told herself severely, you've been sent down here to do a job, and you've done it. Pack your bags and go home. Think about the next job. Forget about this one. You've done what was asked of you—more, even, if you can believe what everyone's telling you—so you can leave here with flags flying high, drums beating thumpety-thump, and bugles blowing too if you want, and everyone will love you for it.

She considered it.

Yes, her inner voice continued, you can go back home and be a hero—or is that heroine? Mr. Roxlet will send you on more assignments like this because you've done so well the first time. Maybe next time it might be Paris, or even Rome; how would you like *them* apples, Cathy McKinnon?

She brooded over it, gathering anger against her fate.

It's true, you know, her inner voice insisted. What do you care about Robert's farms not making money, or the possibility that Doug McKinnon might be stealing from the co-op that he's supposed to be managing? What business is it of yours? What harm can it do to you? And in any case, it will all be solved if Cathy married Robert. Because no matter even if her father is stealing, Robert will get it back through Cathy once he's married her.

No, girl, the voice thundered, all you care about is doing a good job and doing it quickly, smartly and professionally. There's nobody going to be able to say you haven't done that. You can leave here anytime you want, now. The job's done, and done well. Let the people who live here take care of their own problems. Especially Robert. If he's such a fool as to marry that McKinnon creature, the daughter of a penny-pinching old Scottish miser who is also probably a clever thief; if he's foolish enough to let himself fall into her hands—their hands!— then so be it. It's no concern of yours. Let him fall into their hands and handle his own problems.

The voice became wheedling, insidious, very convincing.

Life is pretty good now, right? it said. This is only the first assignment, and it's been a lot of fun, oh, a *lot* of fun. So why give it up? There's lots more fun to come. Who knows where you'll be sent to next? You might even get a name for yourself, like Dino di Cavour, and people might send for you from all over the world, just like they do for him. You could even tie in with Dino, somehow, and work as a team. Can you imagine what that would be like?

But I love Robert Innes, she told the voice. Her heart began to crumble to pieces inside her, now that she'd found the courage to argue with herself. Slow tears started. She closed her eyes to hold them back.

I love him. It doesn't matter if we've only just met, I love him.

She pulled her feet back and dropped her elbows onto her knees, opening her eyes and staring at the red-clay ground through a blur of welling tears. Her sight cleared momentarily as one big drop splashed onto the ground, seeming to stain it a darker red. But new tears blurred her sight again.

Look, she told her inner voice, I know I can't have him. I know Cathy's got him now, that they're going to be engaged, and I know better than you can tell me that I've finished here, and have got to go home again. I know all those things. All I have is the memory of last night, and the fact that I love him.

So what does that mean? said the voice coldly.

It means . . . that I want him . . .

You can't have him.

All right, I know that. I can't have him. But I want the best for him. At least I can get the best for him.

And what does *that* mean?

It means . . . that I think Cathy is wrong for him. He loves his farms. I don't think she even cares about them. He loves this land, this part of the world—it's his *whole* world—and she is a gadabout; sure she's happy to be home now, but in a little while she'll want to go running the roads again, and what do you think that will do to Robert? He'll either have to go with her and leave his farms to someone else to manage or let her go by herself, which is wrong.

She raised her face, staring blurrily at the fence at the end of the court.

Cathy is wrong for Robert. I'm the right person for him and Cathy is definitely the wrong person.

So what are you going to do about it? Are you going to try to stop him marrying Cathy McKinnon? You're a fool if you try.

I don't know. Oh, I don't know. Stop bugging me, won't you!

She started to her feet and almost ran from the court, brushing away the tears, drying her cheeks with her sleeve.

She walked around the deserted grounds until she was quite composed. She stopped crying. She consoled herself over and over with the knowledge that, by accident or intuition, she had somehow managed to do the job that she'd been sent down here to do, and that nobody could take that away from her. Her own convincing words rang hollowly in her ears in any case.

But at last she had calmed herself sufficiently to be able to head back to the manor house and her room. She had analyzed the problem from every angle; she still wasn't sure if she should do anything more than coast for the last day or two, then pack her bags and go home. But she felt able to meet people again, able to show them her own normal face and manner. She wanted time to go upstairs and take a bath, do her hair, and be as attractive and charming as she could possibly manage for dinner

155

tonight. For, after all, if Cathy McKinnon was going to be there, and if Carol Anne figured it was her duty to show her up for what she was, then she'd need every weapon she could get together.

And it *was* her duty. Cathy McKinnon was wrong for Robert; she was as sure of that as she was sure the sun was shining. So Robert had to be shown it as a fact, no matter what it cost.

But she hadn't counted on meeting anyone before she got to her room. Standing at the top of the creaking steps into the manor house as she got to them was the Captain.

"My dear? Is anything wrong?" His voice was full of concern. He started to come down the steps to meet her.

Carol Anne flashed a smile at him. "No, of course not," she assured him. She took his arm when she came abreast of him, and turned him around. He walked up the steps with her, trying to look at her face.

"I was just looking for you, m'dear; wanted to show you the new bar list. Printer sent it this afternoon. But I don't want to add to your troubles, m'dear."

"Why should you think I've got troubles?" They were in the cool darkness of the lounge now.

"If you'll forgive an old man for saying so, well, it looks as if you've been crying, m'dear." He stopped, trying to turn her to look into her face. "Is there anything I can do to help?" His manner was so kind and sympathetic Carol Anne felt the tears starting again. She hurriedly let go of his arm and rushed past him toward the grand stairway. "No. I'm just fine," she blurted over her shoulder.

There was no sanctuary even in her room. Charlene was there with a big smile of welcome which fell to pieces the moment she saw Carol Anne's face. Without saying a word, Carol Anne dashed for the bathroom and locked the door.

She looked in the mirror and saw the streaks her dusty sleeve had made when she wiped the tears away. "Oh,

156

no," she said in a mournful voice. "Why didn't I take an ad in the newspaper and tell everyone in the world?"

There was a gentle tap at the door. "Are you all right, miss?"

"I'm fine thanks, Charlene. I'm just fine." Inspiration came to her. "I barked my shin just as I was coming up the steps, and it made the tears come."

"Oh." Charlene sounded relieved, but she didn't hear her going away from the door.

"Miss, would you like for me to look at it? Perhaps I can put on a bandage."

"No, it's fine, Charlene, I'll be all right." Why couldn't everyone go away and leave her alone? She stayed before the mirror, clutching the edges of the sink, and waited until she heard Charlene's footsteps going away. It seemed an eternity. *Why does everyone have to be so nice? Can't they see I want to be alone?*

She ran the bathwater and slowly got undressed.

Lying in the warm water, soaking away her emotions, she tried to be practical. The alternatives posed by her situation were clear and plain: She could pack up and leave, including leaving Robert to his fate, or she could stay a day or two longer with the intention of trying to save Robert from disaster. Those were the choices.

If she chose the first course, she'd win automatically. Mr. Roxlet would be happy, the Captain would be happy, Cathy McKinnon would be pleased, and even Robert would be happy, at least until being married to Cathy began to show itself up for the disaster it was bound to be. And as for her, why, her life would go on. In time, with luck, she'd get over Robert. Her job and its prospects would improve. She'd have the world at her feet. A good salary, plenty of traveling to adventurous-sounding places, one of the most interesting jobs in the world. She was healthy, and young still. Life would be very sweet, and all she had to do was accept the present situation and live with it.

But if she took the second alternative, everything was a pure gamble. Her only hope of winning was if she could convince Robert that he'd be be making a mistake in marrying Cathy. But even if she did convince him, he wouldn't thank her for it. More likely he would be angry at her for ruining his proposed marriage. He'd think of her as nosy, to say the least. He might even think she'd done it in hopes of furthering her own chances. Which of course was stupid, because whatever happened, she would have to leave the manor house in a day or two.

Slowly she began to lather her arms, hardly aware of what she was doing.

But she'd save Robert's future happiness by doing so. He'd lose his beloved farms if she didn't. Cathy McKinnon would bankrupt him, in time. He'd end up penniless, and Cathy would probably divorce him as soon as his bank account was gone.

But how to prove that this was so?

There was only one way; she would have to find out how Doug McKinnon was cheating the other farmers, and show that Cathy was living her luxurious life on the proceeds of what he was stealing. Because that *had* to be where she was getting all her money.

So how did he do it?

Without having made any conscious decision, without having deliberately chosen one alternative over the other, Carol Anne was already embarked on the second of them, the gamble, the choice that she knew, deep down, could only lead to heartbreak for her, but which she also knew was right and what she had to do. She never even considered the first alternative again.

How did McKinnon steal money from the other farmers?

The question puzzled her brain so much that she forgot where she was until the water began to grow cold around her. Reluctantly she got out of the tub and began to dry herself.

158

Chapter Nine

Carol Anne dressed quickly. She let Charlene do her hair so that she could concentrate on her makeup while it was being done. Charlene just brushed it and brushed it, making it silky soft, letting it hang down Carol Anne's back. She took scissors and trimmed off a snip here and there at the bottom. Carol Anne wore her lavender dress, her best summer one, and her sling-back shoes. She knew she looked her best dressed like this; not too formal, as for a dance, but not too casual either. Cool and neat, she reminded herself.

She wanted to get down to the Captain's office before he left it. Or at least to catch him long enough before dinner so that she could talk to him alone for a while.

She was lucky. He was still in his office. She'd guessed that he spent most of his afternoons there after he'd had his after-lunch siesta.

"My dear, you look charming." He closed the ledger he'd been studying. "What can I do for you? Shall we go into the bar?"

"I'd rather sit here, if we could." The Captain looked slightly disappointed. But Carol Anne knew there was too much chance of meeting Robert if they went to the bar. She took the seat in front of the desk.

"Captain Innes? Do you honestly think I've done a good job here, for you and the hotel?"

"But I've already told you so." He threw his hands wide in perplexity. "A marvelous job. Gave me ideas and gave me heart. Even swung young Robert over to our side."

"Do you think I learned quickly, considering I've only been a travel agent for a month?"

"Amazingly so. Why, child, are you worried about something?"

"Yes. I am. But it's maybe none of my business. So I want to be sure that you trust me."

"Trust you, my dear? With my very life. Truly."

She had been sitting forward on the edge of her chair, her hands on the edge of the desk. Now she leaned back, settled farther into her chair and crossed her knees. This next question had to be handled with the most careful delicacy.

"Captain Innes . . . I'm sure the hotel will make money. And I know—or I think I know—what you want that money for." She looked into his eyes. His eyebrows were drawing closer together, as they always did when he was puzzled. But he didn't say anything, so she drew a breath and carried on.

"I think you want to let Robert have that money so that he can keep the farms operating. Have I guessed right?"

He nodded slowly, his eyebrows still close together, before he spoke. "Yes," he admitted, "something like that."

"Well, what I'm thinking, and I hope you don't get mad at me, is that it won't help Robert." She rushed to get the next words out, giving him no chance to interject. "The farms are losing money, all right. But it won't help to pour extra money into them. You've got to know *why* they're losing money and—"

"But I've told you why already; it's the damned commodities market; it's never paying high prices when we have to sell. At least not high enough prices. They go

160

zooming up after we've sold our crops. Even if we hold off and wait till prices rise, we never seem to hit the peak. All one awful gamble, I assure you. McKinnon himself can't get the hang of it any better than the rest of us, and he's the one who has to keep track of it. Damned market goes up and down—it's the brokers themselves who manipulate it. Doug explained it to us. But we're stuck with them."

She let him talk his puzzlement out, waiting. Every question was important; every answer he gave was valuable.

"Captain. I've told you I'm a bookkeeper. I . . ." She could see the ledgers on the shelf behind the Captain, itched to get her fingers on the one on his desk. But some intuition warned her that it was too soon to ask for permission to do that. She altered the words she was about to say. "I think there's a more important reason why the farms aren't paying; I don't think you're getting full value for your produce."

"But I know we aren't. Know it all too well. It's those blighters in the brokerage offices. Thieves, the whole lot of 'em."

"I think there might be another reason."

"Oh? What?"

"I'm not too sure. But I'm pretty sure I know where I can find out, if you'll let me." Now was the time to ask; now or never. She glanced instinctively at the row of ledgers behind the Captain's head. He caught the glance, and turned to look. Then he laughed.

"Aha," he roared, slapping the ledger on the table in front of him. His eyebrows had separated at last. "I see what you're getting at. Wondered, for a moment. But it's my bookkeeping, right?" He didn't give her time to answer. "Well, that's very nice of you, m'dear. A charming thought. You want to show me some modern system and help me cut my work down, is it? But I couldn't think of it. Have a system already. Not a good one, perhaps, but it works. The books always balance out,

161

after a while." He took the ledger from the desk, stood up, and put it with the others. "It's really very thoughtful of you, my dear, to offer to help. But I want you to enjoy yourself these last few days. Take a holiday, have some fun for a change. Couldn't possibly let you bury your nose in those old account books. Heavens no." He came around to her chair, proffering his arm. "Now. Shall we go into the bar? I'm told there's quite a few people coming to dinner tonight. Just like the old times—except that they'll pay, of course. Gives me quite a funny feeling, having people pay for their dinner in my house. But we have to move with the times."

But Carol Anne stayed in her chair. She was so determined to find out what she wanted to know that she was trembling. She couldn't have got up just then even if she'd wanted to.

"Captain," she blurted out, "I think your farm profits are being siphoned away, somehow. I'm sure of it. And I'm sure I can find out how it's done if you'll only let me help you with the accounts." She looked up at him, tears of frustration about to brim over. "I *know* you're being cheated. I even think I know how, in a rough sort of way. But I can't prove it until I've checked everything."

He stopped and stared. This time his eyebrows rose up on his forehead. Carol Anne almost laughed hysterically at the sight. But she forced herself to stay under control.

There were two or three other chairs in the small room. The Captain took one and pulled it close to Carol Anne, sitting down.

"I don't understand," he said at last, shaking his head slowly.

She laid a hand on his arm. "Captain, it is totally impossible that such a large, well-run estate as this one could be losing money when—"

"Not *losing* money, m'dear. Never said we were *losing* money. Just barely making ends meet; been that way for years."

"Even that. The estate should be coining money, es-

162

pecially in these days of food shortages." He nodded in agreement.

"True," he said. "True. Go on."

"Therefore, as I see it, the estate's profits are being siphoned off somehow. And—"

"Those beastly brokers. Already told you."

She wished he wouldn't interrupt. It was hard enough trying to say what had to be said. But obviously he himself had thought over this same problem and come to his own conclusions, so now he naturally wanted her to agree to them. She considered what he'd said.

"All right," she admitted. "It could be the brokers. What brokers do you use?"

"Used to use them catch as catch can, when we started the co-op. Then McKinnon found a good one in Europe—London, actually—and we've stuck with him for the last few years."

"Who is it?"

"Ian Scott Associates Limited. Why do you ask? The fellows are no better or worse than any other brokers." He patted her hand, which was still on his arm, and smiled. "I know exactly what you're thinking, my dear. Exactly. Puzzled over that same thing, time and time again. But there's no answer to it. None that I can see, anyway." He got to his feet again, chuckling. "My dear Miss Todd, you're an angel. I'll write your Mr. Roxlet and tell him so, be damned if I don't. Not only come down here and fix up our hotel problems, but right after that you want to help us fix up the farm problems." He laughed aloud, once more proffering his arm. "But there you can't help us, m'dear. Robert and I have investigated every possible thing, and it's just beyond us. Not just Robert and I. All the other twenty farmers in the co-op—"

"Twenty?" Carol Anne got to her feet at last, still trembling slightly, but smiling now, putting a good face on this defeat. She'd learn what she had to some other way. "How much land would twenty farms consist of, here in the Mandeville co-op?"

163

"Oh, forty thousand acres or so, give or take." They walked toward the bar, already hearing the sound of voices. "Lots of guests here tonight. Mandeville crowd, mostly. Plus one or two visitors to Mandeville. Be nice to make a small profit."

His mind, she realized, had dismissed the problem of the farms. There was no use in trying to continue their discussion along those lines now. Evidently he thought her quite unable to help.

Well, we shall see about that, she thought grimly, while making small talk as they entered the room where everyone was gathered before dinner.

There were almost twenty people in the bar, but it was such a big room it wasn't crowded. Harry was there, already coming forward to greet her with that flashing smile on his handsome face. Dino was there. Cathy McKinnon was holding court, standing near the bar itself, surrounded by excited young men all eager to voice an opinion on what she'd just said. And Robert was part of the crowd around Cathy, she saw at once.

There were couples seated cozily, talking and smiling in low voices. One larger group of five people around another low table. She and the Captain stopped at the entrance to survey the scene just as Harry came up.

"I don't recognize the manor house anymore," he cried. "It's just marvelous what you've done here. Let me buy you a drink."

"In me own house? Don't be a fool, man. I'll buy the drinks." The smile on the Captain's face was broad. "What will you have, m'dear?" He signaled a waiter. There were four waiters working in the bar tonight, all looking as excited and pleased as the guests.

"Shall we sit over here?" Harry led Carol Anne to a comfortable couch, sitting next to her. Dino came wandering over, drink in hand.

"Hello, Miss Todd," he said mournfully, his eyes on

164

Harry. "I think we can pronounce the bar a success, don't you?"

"It's a much better watering hole than Fred Taylor's old boozer," Harry agreed, nodding vigorously, "even if he has painted it and cleaned it up."

"Glad you like it, m'boy," the captain grunted as he sat, having finished with the waiter. But he immediately got up again. "There's old Ben Wycks, by gad. Haven't seen him in my house in donkey's years. Must go say hello to him. Excuse me, m'dear." Harry looked pleased, and Dino sat facing them both.

"It really is a nice bar," said Harry. "Though I'm damned if I know where he got the money to build it. *And* the pool."

"He's paid my bill," Dino argued. "Got the check on Monday." He set down his drink. "I've already invested it in—"

"You've hardly touched your drink," Harry said, ignoring Dino completely. "Don't you like it? Shall I get you something else?"

"Yes. Please. I'd like a . . . something stronger," Carol Anne answered, thinking she might need it to get her through the rest of the evening.

"Yes, as I was saying," Dino continued, unruffled, "I got my check on Monday and I've already invested it in Cathy's little brokerage company." Carol Anne's ears twitched upright. She was about to blurt something out but managed to hold her tongue, then asked nonchalantly, "Oh, you know about Cathy's firm?"

"Oh, dear," Dino said nervously, his eyes darting about to see if anyone was near, "Cathy asked me to keep it hush-hush, otherwise everyone in the valley would want to get in on it. I haven't lost a penny with her yet."

Carol Anne's mind raced, fitting this latest piece of information into the pattern of knowledge: Cathy wanting to keep her role in the company a secret; Cathy, her father, and a still-unidentified third man in partnership.

165

Plus Cathy's father just happening to find the Ian Scott brokerage firm for the farmer's co-op. Struggling to control her rising excitement, she leaned closer to Dino, suggesting that she too was a part of the secret.

"You don't have to worry about me," she said quietly. "I understand Cathy and her father are doing quite well."

A sigh of relief escaped Dino's lips. "Oh, yes, yes. Cathy's company is the best broker I've found, and—"

Carol Anne couldn't sit still any longer and wait for Dino to say what she wanted to hear. She decided to make a wild guess.

"Her firm is Ian Scott Associates, isn't it?" she murmured.

"The very same. Do you play the market too?" Dino asked, reaching for his near-empty glass.

Now it all fitted into place. How could Dino be making money from the very same firm the co-op farmers invested with unless something crooked was going on? Now Carol Anne knew why Doug McKinnon had enough money to buy up land from the other farmers, who weren't doing so well. He was not only acting as manager of the co-op, but by being a part-owner of the brokerage house that handled the co-op's business, he made money there, too. Plenty of money, by the sound of Cathy's expensive tastes.

Her excitement at the discovery she'd made began to evaporate. Her wildly beating heart slowed down. She felt her shoulders drop as she realized she was really no farther ahead. All she had was Dino's guarded admission about the owners of Ian Scott Associates and a few words said at the pool by a drowsy Cathy. She had no real proof; it would be her word against Cathy's, for she could not put too much faith in Dino.

Carol Anne's mind was awhirl. She hardly heard anything that Dino said to her, but fortunately Harry chose that time to return with her drink, thus saving her from having to pursue the conversation with Dino any further.

166

Harry came with a martini for her and big white smile. "You look terribly sad," he sympathized. "Drink up and you'll feel much better."

She did so unthinkingly, downing the martini as if it was water, not tasting it until she took the glass from her lips.

"Wow!" said Harry in an awed voice.

"Ahhhhhh . . ." was the only sound a pop-eyed Carol Anne could manage as she tried to catch her breath. Weakly she reached out and clung to Harry's arm.

"That wasn't lemonade, you know." His voice was full of concern as he braced himself under her steely grip.

"Ahhhhhhhhh . . ." said Carol Anne again, squeezing until he winced.

Then suddenly she felt enormously better. She smiled like the rising sun. The concern vanished from Harry's face.

"You could let go of me now, if you like," he suggested.

"Whoops. Sorry, Harry." She did let go, patting his shoulder where she'd gripped it so hard. "What was that, a martini? I've never had a martini before. They're very nice. May I have another?"

"No. Heavens no! It hurts me when you drink martinis." He rubbed the sore spot on his shoulder, grinning at her. "Wouldn't you like to have dinner now, instead?"

"Dinner?" She thought about it seriously. "Are you sure I couldn't have another—?"

"Quite sure," he said firmly, taking her arm. The dinner gong sounded as he did so. "There, you see? Everybody's going into the dining room now. Let's hurry and get a good table."

Everyone in the bar was rising or heading toward the door, the ladies with their arms linked through the men's. Harry and Carol Anne led the procession. He found them a table and pulled out Carol Anne's chair.

"Whoops," she said as she sat. The room seemed to be spinning. She had to clutch the table edge for support. She didn't let go even after she was in her seat. What had happened to the room? She squeezed her eyes closed, trying to make it stop. When she opened them, she saw Cathy McKinnon. Firmly she closed her eyes again.

"Hello, Carol Anne. I missed you in the bar." The voice was Robert's, and it sounded cool. She opened her eyes to see him just about to sit down, his face expressionless. He was facing her at the table. Cathy was on her right, and Harry on her left.

Harry was studying the wine list, but Robert was studying Carol Anne, his face still expressionless, though it seemed to Carol Anne to be somewhat darker than normally. But that could be because, though the room was no longer spinning, everything seemed to be slightly out of focus. Maybe she was imagining that his face looked darker. And his eyes; why was he looking at her so sternly? But he did look handsome, even so.

"What do we say to a bottle of red?" Harry asked as an anxious-looking waiter hovered over his shoulder, waiting to hear what people thought of the suggestion. Carol Anne nodded, as did everyone else. Harry talked to the waiter, handing him the list.

"Robert and I met on the road this morning, quite by chance," said Cathy. "We went riding together."

Robert chuckled. "You mean you hung around and got in my way while I was trying to get my work done, don't you?"

"Oh, you old grouch. Don't you ever stop work long enough to have a little fun? I can see I'll have to take you in hand." The proprietory tone of Cathy's voice set Carol Anne's teeth on edge.

"Life can't be all fun," Robert argued. "Work first; fun afterward."

"Well, darling"—Cathy patted his hand—"work's over with for today at least, so let's have some fun. What are we going to eat?"

Robert picked up a menu and opened it. "Well, let's see, now . . ." Cathy turned her smiling face to Carol

168

Anne. "Can you order for yourself, dear? Or would you rather let Harry do it for you?" She kept her voice down so only Carol Anne could hear.

Anger bubbled up inside her. She forced a sweet smile onto her face. "Such a pity they don't have crow on the menu," she began. Cathy interrupted, "But, darling, you've eaten it already today. Don't be greedy, dear." Again they spoke in low voices so that only they could hear, making sure to be smiling at all times.

"How about the vichyssoise to begin with?" asked Robert.

"Sounds delicious, darling, simply divine."

"And after that, perhaps the escargots?"

"I never could stand them, dear; may I skip the snails?"

"As you wish, Cathy. What are you having, Carol Anne?"

"I think I'll let Harry decide." Harry was studying the menu. "It's so much easier that way." What did Robert think he had at this table, a harem?

She looked away from the table so that she could blink away the starting tears. Through the blur she saw the Captain seated with some older people at a nearby table. Dino was at another table, with three men all together, and only one girl, a young and giggly thing whom Dino totally ignored. She looked up as the waiter came back with the wine Harry had ordered.

She sipped her glass when it was filled. It didn't taste like anything special, and Harry had gone to such trouble over it. But she was thirsty, so she drained her glass.

"Tell us about this wonderful antique sale you're planning, Robert." Cathy's voice was comfortably possessive, as if she was coaxing a favorite child to do his party piece.

"It's Carol Anne's idea, not mine. You tell us, Carol Anne."

"Oh, well. Antiques fetch high prices these days. And since the manor house is full of antiques, I thought the

169

other houses in the valley might have a lot too. So it seemed like a good idea to combine a worldwide antique sale with the hotel's grand opening. That's all."

"But that isn't all, darling. As I understand it, the proceeds from the hotel will be enough to build dozens and dozens of cottages somewhere on the grounds. Am I not right?" Cathy's face, for once, had lost its smile. She seemed genuinely interested in hearing more. So Carol Anne nodded agreement. But that didn't satisfy Cathy. "And with so many cottages, the hotel's bound to be a roaring success, is it not?" Again Carol Anne nodded. Cathy smiled, raising her glass. "Then here's to the jolly old antique sale. May it bring in tons of money." She drank half the glass, then turned to Robert. "Darling, you simply *must* let me help. I think it will be just super to go prowling around all the other houses in the valley and dig out their old furniture, then sell it to rich Americans for exorbitant prices." Her tone was now wheedling and girlish. Carol Anne felt ill.

But Robert was surprisingly firm. "No, Cathy. It's Carol Anne's show. I want her to handle it her own way. If she wants you to help, she can ask you."

Waiters arrived, bringing soup. Harry had also ordered the vichyssoise for Carol Anne and himself. He refilled her glass of wine, and she sipped it instead of eating the cold soup, which she found she didn't care for.

Carol Anne wanted to go home. She just wanted to get inside her own little apartment in downtown Toronto, close the door and sit there in the dark and cry. Never in her life had she felt so low. The fact that she was in a glittering dining room with a handsome man on a warm tropical island, being served exotic dishes and rare wines, with the promise of an evening of gaiety and wit and laughter ahead, meant less than nothing to her. All that mattered was that Robert was sitting opposite her, chatting happily with beautiful Cathy McKinnon, whom he was planning to marry. She would never even see him

170

again, after Sunday at the latest. And between now and then, whenever she did see him, it would probably be in the company of the woman he was going to marry—the same woman who was living off the profits he worked on his land so hard to make, and who no doubt viewed the coming success of the hotel as yet one more source of income to appease her expensive appetites. Carol Anne decided, woozily—for the wine, added to the martini, was affecting her—to test her theory about Cathy's plans for the hotel.

"Will you be staying in Mandeville, Cathy, now that you're back?"

"But this is my home, darling. One needs a home."

"But will you stay home?"

"Who knows? It all depends." Cathy seemed to be on her guard, for some reason. Carol Anne decided on a different tack.

"You would miss all the fun of traveling." she mused, "and all the friends you've made in Europe."

"But if the hotel is a success, they'll be coming here, darling. So I won't miss them, will I?"

"But surely you'll want to travel sometimes?" Carol Anne pressed further.

"Of course, darling. Doesn't everyone?" Cathy said gaily, then turned to the others at the table to end the conversation.

This was leading nowhere. Cathy was being too guarded, answering her questions with questions of her own. Not to be denied, Carol Anne suddenly decided to change tactics and strike for home. Swallowing the lump in her throat and trying to sound casual, Carol Anne remarked, "But Cathy, what about your business? Surely you'll want to keep track of it?"

For the first time the entire evening Cathy was visibly shaken, her cool exterior shattered, and Robert's eyes darted from one woman to the other but finally rested on Carol Anne. His eyes were openly hostile, sending a chill through her. Carol Anne tore her eyes from his and concentrated on the clearly distraught Cathy.

"Why, I don't know what you're talking about, dear," she managed to say in a shaky voice as she toyed with the stem of her wineglass.

This was the moment Carol Anne was waiting for; surely with just a little more persistence she would crack.

"Oh, you know, the firm you and your father and—"

Cathy turned her back to Robert and glared at Carol Anne. "You *must* be mistaken," she said firmly.

"Oh, but—" Before Carol Anne could finish her sentence, a stern male voice interrupted.

"I believe you *are* mistaken," Robert said slowly and evenly, openly becoming Cathy's ally. He grabbed Cathy from behind and turned her to face him. "You must forgive Carol Anne," he said soothingly. "She's only been here a week and it's only natural that she'd get things confused." Cathy smiled adoringly at Robert and squeezed his hand intimately.

"Thank you, darling," she said sweetly, her confidence and cool reserve once more intact. "I'm sure that's it. The poor girl's just a bit confused," she barely whispered.

Carol Anne was stunned! The main course was brought to the table, but she neither knew nor cared what it was. She wanted to run from the table—from Cathy's triumphant smiles and Robert's indifference—but she would not give either of them that satisfaction. She made a pretense of eating, smiled whenever anyone looked her way and managed to say a word or two when it was demanded. Once during the meal her eyes met Robert's, and the memories of the intimate moments they had shared flashed before her, sending a flush of color to her face. She was certain he knew the turmoil she was feeling at that very moment, but his eyes registered no emotion, and finally they looked away from one another.

Finally the coffee was served, and having drunk the almost scalding liquid, she was quick to seize an excuse to leave the table. She only wanted to get away from them

172

all. She'd give anything to be home in snowy Toronto right now.

The scent of frangipani rose up shyly from the garden, bathing her in unwarranted nostalgia. A week ago she'd not even have recognized it; tonight it evoked memories. She tried to see Find-your-man Hill from where she stood, but there were too many trees in the way. So she walked slowly down the creaking steps into the courtyard.

Her steps took her toward the little hill, but she stopped in the ornamental garden under the spreading mango tree; surely on such a generously gorgeous night there might be other people there, and she didn't want to disturb them.

The one tall lamp shed its light, but off to one side was the magnificent yellow moon, already grown more full and beautiful. The night insects sang their praises to her, chirruping and clicking, keening and ticking.

She stared at the moon, trying to imagine men up there, but unable to believe the fact. The moon was inviolate, serene, eternally floating in peace; men could not have disturbed her.

She stood still, letting her shocked senses calm themselves. How could Robert be a part of the McKinnons' deception? She knew he wanted the estate to be prosperous, but at such a price! Yet she had heard him with her own ears. Willfully she struggled to erase all thought of the nightmarish evening. Her eyes fixed on the golden glow in space, she slowly achieved a form of peace and didn't hear the soft footfalls on the grass as they approached her. She didn't know she wasn't alone until she felt a hand on her arm.

She whirled around with fear-widened eyes. Her hand reached for her mouth. Robert stood next to her. The person most responsible for her torment and humiliation.

"What the hell did you think you were doing back there?" he said angrily.

She began to laugh. She had to force herself to stop, afraid of becoming hysterical. His voice was husky and deep, but now, without anger, he continued, "I've wanted to talk to you all evening." He took his hand away from her arm, but the warmth of it was still there.

Carol Anne closed her eyes. She would not allow him to come to her now. He had had his chance inside, but he was too busy playing the white knight in shining armor for Cathy. She would not give him the chance of knowing how much he had hurt her then or now. "Robert, I'm going home soon. You'll be staying here with Cathy." She kept her voice under control.

"We've got to talk," he muttered.

"I've done my work," she continued, as if she didn't hear him. "I have no more reason to stay here." She laughed again, softly though. "Cathy McKinnon will soon make you forget I was ever here at all."

Once again his anger rose. "I have no intention of forgetting." He took her arm, quickly guiding her toward the gap in the hedge to the shimmering translucent pool.

They stopped, as they had last night, saying nothing. Then she felt the pressure on her arm that warned he wished to lead her away. But suddenly anger developed within her. Was he planning a repeat of that long ago evening, step by step? How dare he, after he'd humiliated her and now that he and Cathy were engaged?

"We won't be going to Find-your-man Hill," she said coldly. "Not tonight. Nor any other night." She shrugged free of his hand. .

"Carol Anne"—he said her name firmly, trying to control the rising emotion in his voice—"don't say anything you might regret later."

She might regret! What right had he to say that to her after tonight? His attitude only made her angrier still. The emotion boiled up inside her and exploded at last.

"You're a fool! You're slaving night and day for the farm and getting nothing out of it. Now you're going to lose the work your father and I have put into the hotel, and I don't want to be here to see it happen." Carol Anne had never felt such anger before, and she struggled to control her trembling body. "It'll break the Captain's heart, and you don't even know that everything he's been doing—yes, the whole hotel idea—is strictly for your benefit. He no more wanted to see strangers sleeping in his wife's room than you did. But he's willing to turn his own home into a hotel, just so that he can make enough money for you to keep the estate running. And you never understood. You fought him right down the line!" She was trembling uncontrollably now, but when Robert went to put his arms around her, she frantically hit his arms away.

No one had ever spoken to him like that before, and it took great effort on his part to keep from grabbing her and shaking her soundly. Stuffing his hands in his trouser pockets, he seethed, then spoke. "I know I've given the Captain a hard time, but I've had other things on my mind."

She drew a breath but couldn't bring herself to mention Cathy's name. But her tongue found another way of saying it. "Yes, it's been quite clear all evening that you've had your mind on the same spendthrift cheat who's already cheated you and the other farmers out of all your profits."

Robert uttered an epithet that shocked her, and grabbed her arms. "What are you trying to say? What do you know?"

"Cathy," she spat. "Cathy McKinnon, who's going to marry you! She and her father are partners in Ian Scott Associates."

His fingers squeezed into her flesh. "You little fool! I know that, and tonight you almost ruined everything!"

He knew? All along he knew! She had suffered over how to tell him that his beloved was a cheat, and he knew all along. Carol Anne tore from his grasp and with volcanic rage slapped his face soundly, then sped away.

Carol Anne got up from the bed, her face tearstained and her makeup ruined. She'd been lying there ever since she'd rushed into the room. It seemed like hours ago, but

175

faintly she could still hear voices from the bar downstairs. So it couldn't have been so very long.

She opened armoire after armoire until she found her two suitcases, and when she did, for a moment she smiled. Charlene had obviously washed the dust off them. It was a wonder she hadn't starched them too. Carol Anne sighed. She never had got around to telling Charlene about the starch, and now it looked as if she never would be able to.

She opened the suitcases on the bed's counterpane, then slowly opened drawers, finding her things, all washed and clean now, thanks to Charlene, and packed them away. Maybe she could write Charlene a letter about the starch.

She took her dresses off the hangers in the armoire and packed them too, folding them carefully. Her heavy winter coat she put on the bed beside the cases; she'd need that soon enough. Her boots? She'd fold them once; stick them in her small overnight luggage and carry them.

At last, except for the things she planned to wear and the clothes she was already wearing, she was all packed.

One last bath? No, but a quick wash and new makeup, at least. She'd last till she got home.

Home. Visions of an overheated apartment smelling stale after her absence. Of frozen people hurrying along icy streets. Were there really places like that? But of course there were. And they were the *real* places, where real people lived. This was all make-believe, here in Mandeville.

She went into the bathroom and washed her face, slipping out of her clothes, almost hanging them on the door hook out of newly acquired force of habit for Charlene to look after. But she took them out when she was washed and dry, and packed them away, locking her suitcases with a final-sounding click-click, click-click.

She opened the door a bit, listening. The guests were still downstairs. Well, it was now or never. She descended the grand staircase, dressed in a beige knit shirtwaist dress with a matching jacket. She'd be warm enough against the

176

cool evening air, and once she arrived in Toronto, she'd simply have to exchange her tan sling-backed sandals for her boots, slip on her winter coat, and she'd be ready to face the cold weather.

At the entrance to the bar she stopped. Just as she'd imagined, everyone had finished dinner, and most of the guests had come back into the bar. The giggly girl that Dino had been so studiously ignoring earlier was playing the piano, and doing it well. She'd gathered most of the young guests around her to sing along with her tunes. Dino stood to one side, a drink in his hand, looking bored. He saw her come to the door. She signaled him over.

"Dino? Do you have a car?" she asked when he came near. He nodded, then sipped his drink. "Yes. I rented a Jag at the airport. Do you want to go somewhere?"

Now it was her turn to nod. "I want to go home," she said simply. Then she looked over his shoulder into the bar. There was no sign of Robert or Cathy. Nor of the Captain. She would have liked to say good-bye to the old man and explain why she was leaving in such a rush, but it was too late now. Harry was with the group singing by the piano and didn't notice her there.

She looked back at Dino. "Will you do me that big favor? Drive me to the airport? Please? I've just got to get away from here as quickly as I can."

"All the way to the airport?" Dino mused. "Well, if this party had any life to it, I'd probably say no. But it's dead, just dead on its feet. So I might as well, I suppose." He felt in his jacket pockets and found his car keys. "Where are your bags?"

"Still in my room."

Dino looked around, caught the eye of one of the waiters and called him over, giving him instructions about the bags.

"Do you want to say good-bye to anyone?"

"No. If you come back, will you give the Captain my apologies for leaving like this? Tell him I'll write him a letter."

177

They left the manor house together.

His car was one of the low twelve-cylinder sports models of the Jaguar line. Dino was evidently very pleased with it. "Not a patch on my own Ferrari in Rome, of course," he admitted, "but quite a nice little car."

When the waiter brought the luggage, they had a problem. Only one bag would fit in the trunk. But they managed to wedge the smaller one behind Carol Anne's seat at last. Even though it took some time, nobody came down the creaking wooden stairs and saw them. The singing from the bar was loud and tuneful on the night air, counterpointed by the song of the crickets in the bushes. Everyone must be still in there. Everyone except Robert and Cathy. Firmly she closed her mind to such thoughts.

Just as they were getting into the car, a tiny gnome of a black man appeared, carrying a shotgun. Carol Anne remembered him instantly. But his name refused to come into her mind. Then she got it, just as he came to the side of the car.

"Watson?" she smiled. "You *are* Watson?"

"Yes, miss, Watson, the night watchman. I watch to see nobody steal the cars or anything."

"I wondered why I never saw you again. . . ."

Dino started the powerful engine with an organlike roar, drowning out the possibility of any further conversation. Watson held his gun like a stick and waved it, smiling hugely, enjoying the sound of the Jaguar's engine. Carol Anne waved at him as they pulled away.

They zoomed down the driveway so fast that Carol Anne had to hang on despite the fact that she was already seat-belted in. By the time he hit the straight stretch leading toward the local village, Dino was doing eighty, climbing rapidly to ninety. Carol Anne's hair was streaming in the warm wind of their passing. She tried to hold it down with one hand.

Even when they came to the two wooden bridges, Dino didn't slow down; he flashed over them so fast the car almost flew. And as for slowing down through the village!

178

If anything, he went faster—three chickens in the road, still up and about far too long after dark for their own good, fluttered into the air with indignant squawks. Luckily there were no children about.

Dino drove terrifyingly, imperiously, scaring Carol Anne rigid. The noise of their passage prevented speech, let alone conversation. Even though she was terrified, there was nothing useful she could do or say about it. In any case, it took all her energy just to hang on, and at least she didn't think of Robert and his deception. All she had in mind was getting to the airport in one piece. She'd never in her life even imagined there could be such a reckless driver. When she wasn't hanging on to the car door, she hung on to her winter coat in her lap, and her streaming hair. It felt like it was being pulled slowly out by the roots.

Dino did slow down for Mandeville. At last she was getting a look at this little town. But such a swift look that nothing registered; just a blur of buildings and houses, of neon lights downtown and soft window lights in the outskirts. It could just as well have been Elbow, Saskatchewan or Atlanta, Georgia, for all she was able to notice.

And of course after Mandeville he speeded up again. He went flat out on the straight stretches, and hardly slowed at all for the curves. Her heart was in her mouth so often she was afraid of biting it in two.

But at last even Dino's speed palled. She stopped clutching at the door. She let her hair fly loose and free. As the feeling of freedom and safety came over her, she even had one wild moment when she felt like letting go of her winter coat and seeing it fly into the night and away. She laughed aloud, but it was soundless against the rush and roar of the wind and the motor.

Free. That's what you are, free! she told herself. No ties. No obligations except to your work. No duties except the ones you already learned. The Manor House Hotel is all behind you. It's all over. Forget it forever. Ahead of you there's nothing but life and laughter. . . .

179

But no love, a small voice said.

Phooey! Who needs love?

You do.

Dino was concentrating so carefully on his wild and dangerous driving that he couldn't spare a glance for her, so he didn't notice as the wind whipped the welling tears from her eyes and streamed them in precious droplets in their wake.

Chapter Ten

It had taken Robert Innes over two hours to drive Carol Anne Todd to the Innes estate from the airport. It took Dino di Cavour one hour and seven minutes to drive her back there. She had stopped crying by the time they arrived. She was calm now, bereft of emotions; even Dino's screaming, curving, breakneck charge through Kingston to the airport had done nothing but leave her cold.

"Thank you, Dino," she said demurely when the engine stopped at last. "I really appreciated the ride." Then she remembered how vain he was. "You're the best driver I've ever ridden with. I'm sure nobody else could have made it in such a short time from Mandeville to here."

He glowed with pleasure. "Oh, that was nothing. You should ride with me in my Ferrari."

Her eyes widened involuntarily at the thought. But she quickly got them under control. "Will you be sure and give the Captain my message? Tell him I'm dreadfully sorry to have to leave without saying good-bye, but I got news of something I just had to attend to in Toronto right away."

"There's only the one phone in the manor house," he reminded her, smiling rather cruelly.

"Well, maybe Charlene gave me a message or something," she answered him comfortably. She was so tired. Nothing mattered anymore, not even being nice to Dino.

But he retaliated. He sat in his car while she got her own bags out of the trunk and from behind the seat. She had to put her winter coat on to be able to carry them both. But as soon as she was clear of the car, Dino started the engine.

"Bye," he shouted, waving. "Have a good trip." And before the last word was out of his mouth, he was doing fifty. She stood there listening to the powerful engine accellerating into the dark.

There was nobody inside the airport building except one bored and sleepy passenger agent, to whom Carol Anne handed her ticket.

"The earliest flight is at seven this morning." she told Carol Anne, handing her back the ticket. "Do you have anywhere to stay?"

"Can I sit here in the airport lounge?"

"If you wish. But I can get you a cab into Kingston, if you'd rather. There's lots of hotels."

"No, I think I'll just sit here. Thank you."

She found a long padded bench covered in a thin blue plastic cushion. She sat there staring at the advertisements on the wall ahead of her, feeling so drowsy she couldn't keep her eyes open. There was nobody else in the building at all. Even the bored passenger agent had found some quiet little room somewhere else, and was probably sleeping. Carol Anne's eyelids felt like lead.

She folded her winter coat at last, and made a pillow out of it, then sighed and stretched full length on top of the blue plastic cushion, and closed her eyes gratefully.

Within seconds she was asleep. And she didn't dream. So that it seemed she had only just closed her eyes when she felt herself picked up bodily like a baby and cradled in someone's arms. Her eyes snapped open. For a moment she couldn't remember where she was supposed to be.

"You're coming home. Right now."

182

Robert's face was above hers, only inches away.

He hugged her closer. His strained look vanished and he broke into a smile. "Thank heaven there wasn't a flight tonight."

"Put me down. Put me *down!*" She kicked and struggled, mortified at his presumption. Finally he had to set her down on her feet. But immediately he picked up her two suitcases, once again tucking the little one under his arm and holding onto the bigger one with his hand. He reached out his free hand, trying to catch hold of her shoulder or arm. She ducked out of his way.

"Come on, Carol Anne. Let's get out of here."

Only now did she realize that dawn was breaking and that the airport building was beginning to fill up with sweepers, people arriving for the early-morning flights, passenger agents coming on duty. She must have slept for hours.

"Go away! Put my suitcases down!"

Instead he marched off, still with one under his arm and the other in his hand. He didn't even look over his shoulder to see what she would do. So she had to run after him to save her suitcases.

"Stop! Robert Innes, just you put my luggage down!" She looked frantically around, seeking help. A nearby sweeper was pushing listlessly at his broom, not even looking at what was happening. Carol Anne ran the two paces toward him and grabbed his arm.

"See that man!" She pointed dramatically. But Robert was out of sight. With a shriek of frustration she ran in the direction in which he'd gone. The broom pusher looked after her, slack-jawed.

Her frustration boiled over.

"Thief!" she cried. "Stop, thief!" as she ran after Robert's broad back. "That man's stealing my luggage!"

Some of the early-morning arrivals looked up, showing little interest. Most of them pretended they hadn't heard her. Crying in angry frustration, she ran after Robert.

He was already in the parking lot. By the time she

reached him, he was tossing her heavy bags into the back of the old station wagon.

"Give me back my luggage!"

"Get in the car."

"I won't!"

He walked around to the passenger door and opened it.

"In," he said, pointing.

"I . . . will . . . not . . . get . . . in!" she shouted. Robert looked around. People from arriving cars snapped their eyes away when he looked at them. A slow flush began to mount his cheeks. Hunching his shoulders, he marched toward her. She stood her ground.

"One step closer and I'll scream so loud they'll hear me in Canada," she warned him. He stopped.

They stood there, ten feet apart, staring at each other. Carol Anne was breathing so quickly she thought her heart might burst.

"Carol Anne, listen to me. Don't make any noise, just listen to me."

"Swine!" she breathed deeper. "What about Cathy McKinnon?"

He took an even deeper breath. "Carol Anne, can we forget about Cathy McKinnon for a minute?"

She waited for him to continue.

"Please get in." He held the door open for her again.

Carol Anne had never heard that pleading sound in his voice before. She could feel herself weakening, but with her last bit of energy she shook her head vehemently. "Give me back my luggage," she said in a loud voice. "Give it back or I'll make a scene."

In total frustration he slammed closed the car door, and when he spoke, his own voice was loud. But it was also clear, honest, and defiant.

"Carol Anne Todd," he said, "I love you more than anyone or anything, so I won't give you back your suitcases." Carol Anne's heart burst with joy as she listened. "I want to explain everything to you, and I'm going to stand here until you give me a chance, even if you

184

make the biggest scene since the last tropical storm hit this island!" Someone in the small crowd that had been gathering while he spoke gave a cheer. Carol Anne looked wildly about her in embarrassment.

Robert marched toward her with a face like joyful thunder and scooped her up in his arms like a baby. He marched back to the station wagon, got the door open again somehow and leaned in, dropping her on the seat.

"Now, stay there!" he roared as he marched around to the driver's side. Still head-over-heels from the words she had heard, Carol Anne could only gaze at him as he quickly opened his door and slid in beside her.

Robert roared the car back out of its parking space, screeched to a stop, leaned across the seat, pulled Carol Anne to him, gave her an enormous kiss and growled, "I love you. I swear it. Now, fasten your seat belt!"

Then he rammed the gearshift into first and thundered away, to the accompaniment of clapping from those people who had gathered around to witness the earlier quarrel. But after that he said nothing for the longest time while he negotiated the excitingly dangerous early-morning traffic of Kingston, honking at donkey carts, skipping by crazy bicyclists, scraping by approaching speeding cars by fractions of an inch. He said nothing. Terrified of distracting him from his driving, Carol Anne just prayed. But all the time, mixed up among her pleas for a safe journey, were a thousand questions, all presenting themselves to be asked of Robert the minute it was safe to do so. But she was afraid to ask them; he was in such a violent mood. But . . . what about Cathy McKinnon?

It wasn't until they were negotiating the first curve leading up into the already familiar mountains that he spoke. The traffic had thinned out almost to the point of having disappeared. There were few houses near the road. He pointed ahead, laughed unexpectedly and edged to the side of the road.

Carol Anne seized her opportunity now that it was safe.

185

After all, it was all very well for him to come swooping down on her in the airport and carry her off and tell her he loved her. *But what about Cathy McKinnon?*

"What about Cathy McKinnon?" she cried exasperatedly.

The car was hardly moving by now. Robert was able to face her while he answered. His face was serious and grave.

"You nearly ruined everything last night," he said, and his tone of voice made Carol Anne shrink into her seat.

"You came here and by accident discovered things that I knew all along, but had to pretend I didn't, or the ones who were cheating me and the other farmers would have been able to get away."

"I was only trying to help you!" she cried.

"Well, don't be in such a rush in future. Talk to me first. By heavens, I could have choked you last night when you nearly spoiled everything by blurting what you'd found out."

But suddenly he smiled. Then he shook his head.

"Carol Anne, listen." He turned his face to the windshield once more, to make certain they weren't too near the ditch. "I discovered some time ago that Cathy was a partner in Ian Scott Associates," he said slowly. "But *saying* something fradulent is going on and *proving* it are two different things." He turned momentarily to look at Carol Anne, who was dumbfounded at his news.

"I've been waiting for some documents to arrive that would confirm my suspicions about Cathy and her father, but your little display last night precipitated my original plans. Just before you ran away, I went right in and faced Cathy with it in front of everyone in the room. Her father was there too, of course. And when Cathy broke down and admitted it, he tried to deny it, but it was too late. The Captain has been delegated to retain a lawyer and to prefer charges against Ian Scott Associates. The police have been notified, of course, here and in Europe, and the first thing they did was warn Cathy and her father to stay in Mandeville and not try to move away." Robert sighed, the strain of the previous evening showing clearly in his eyes. "They're both under a sort of house arrest. Cathy was furious."

He stopped the car, then turned toward her. "Carol Anne Todd, there never was any woman in my life until you came along. Cathy never was important to me. Even when we were younger, there was always a competition between us, and whenever she lost, she became nasty. But since you've been at the manor house, it's as if you've been here all the time and I've known you all my life. And yet I know so little about you." She could see it wasn't easy for him to admit these things to her and she loved him even more for doing so. "Before I even met you I had made up my mind to ignore you and your reason for being here." He reached over and took her hand in his. "But from the moment I saw you at the airport, so neat and cool, you caught my eye and I knew you were very special." He gestured at the ditch at the side of the road. "Remember this spot?" he asked. Carol Anne looked about her, wondering. Then suddenly it came to her.

"The donkey!" she said, smiling. "This is where we hit the donkey."

"That's right; it was just about here. And it was right here that I realized you were the woman for me. You didn't scream and panic when we had that accident; you didn't hide in the car. Most other women would have done something silly like that. . . ."

"Oh, I don't know. All women aren't—"

"Well, maybe you're right," he broke in. "But like I told you already, I've never had much to do with women; I've been too busy working. Cathy McKinnon was just about the only woman I ever spent any time with, and I'm sure she isn't typical. No, I watched you from the moment we met, and when I learned from Watson, the night watchman, that you'd run off to the airport in Dino's car, it felt as if my heart was being torn out of me. I just had to

187

follow you, to bring you back." He was smiling. "I just can't imagine the old manor house without you inside it. I want to be able to look up when I'm in the fields and see you on Find-your-man Hill, looking down at me. Carol Anne Todd, will you marry me?"

And that, Carol Anne realized, was what she had been waiting to hear him say. She hadn't known it in so many words. No voice had whispered it in her ear, but now that she'd heard Robert ask her, she knew that this was the way it had to be; the *only* way it could be between her and him.

"Robert Innes," she said softly, her heart full, "yes, I will."

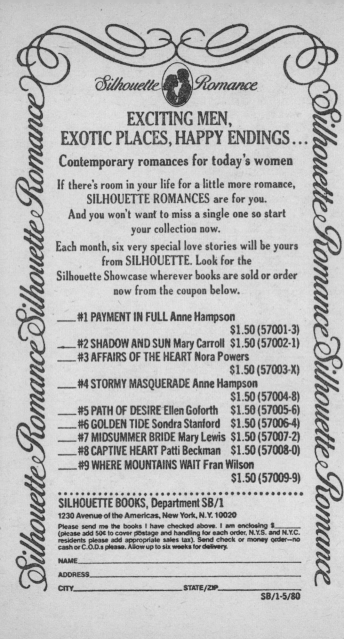